DRIVEN FROM HOME

OR,

CARL CRAWFORD'S EXPERIENCE

I0666985

Horatio Alger, Jr.

1st WORLD
LIBRARY
Literary Society

Driven From Home

Horatio Alger, Jr.

© 1st World Library – Literary Society, 2005
PO Box 2211
Fairfield, IA 52556
www.1stworldlibrary.org
First Edition

LCCN: 2005906497

Softcover ISBN: 1-4218-1553-2
Hardcover ISBN: 1-4218-1453-6
eBook ISBN: 1-4218-1653-9

Purchase *"Driven From Home"*
as a traditional bound book at:
www.1stWorldLibrary.org/purchase.asp?ISBN=1-4218-1553-2

1st World Library Literary Society is a nonprofit
organization dedicated to promoting literacy by:

- Creating a free internet library accessible from any
  computer worldwide.
- Hosting writing competitions and offering book
  publishing scholarships.

Readers interested in supporting literacy
through sponsorship, donations or
membership please contact:
literacy@1stworldlibrary.org
Check us out at: www.1stworldlibrary.ORG
and start downloading free ebooks today.

Driven From Home
contributed by Tim, Ed & Rodney
in support of
1st World Library Literary Society

CHAPTER I

DRIVEN FROM HOME.

A boy of sixteen, with a small gripsack in his hand, trudged along the country road. He was of good height for his age, strongly built, and had a frank, attractive face. He was naturally of a cheerful temperament, but at present his face was grave, and not without a shade of anxiety. This can hardly be a matter of surprise when we consider that he was thrown upon his own resources, and that his available capital consisted of thirty-seven cents in money, in addition to a good education and a rather unusual amount of physical strength. These last two items were certainly valuable, but they cannot always be exchanged for the necessaries and comforts of life.

For some time his steps had been lagging, and from time to time he had to wipe the moisture from his brow with a fine linen handkerchief, which latter seemed hardly compatible with his almost destitute condition.

I hasten to introduce my hero, for such he is to be, as Carl Crawford, son of Dr. Paul Crawford, of Edgewood Center. Why he had set out to conquer fortune single-handed will soon appear.

A few rods ahead Carl's attention was drawn to a

wide-spreading oak tree, with a carpet of verdure under its sturdy boughs.

"I will rest here for a little while," he said to himself, and suiting the action to the word, threw down his gripsack and flung himself on the turf.

"This is refreshing," he murmured, as, lying upon his back, he looked up through the leafy rifts to the sky above. "I don't know when I have ever been so tired. It's no joke walking a dozen miles under a hot sun, with a heavy gripsack in your hand. It's a good introduction to a life of labor, which I have reason to believe is before me. I wonder how I am coming out - at the big or the little end of the horn?"

He paused, and his face grew grave, for he understood well that for him life had become a serious matter. In his absorption he did not observe the rapid approach of a boy some-what younger than himself, mounted on a bicycle.

The boy stopped short in surprise, and leaped from his iron steed.

"Why, Carl Crawford, is this you? Where in the world are you going with that gripsack?"

Carl looked up quickly.

"Going to seek my fortune," he answered, soberly.

"Well, I hope you'll find it. Don't chaff, though, but tell the honest truth."

"I have told you the truth, Gilbert."

With a puzzled look, Gilbert, first leaning his bicycle against the tree, seated himself on the ground by Carl's side.

"Has your father lost his property?" he asked, abruptly.

"No."

"Has he disinherited you?"

"Not exactly."

"Have you left home for good?"

"I have left home - I hope for good."

"Have you quarreled with the governor?"

"I hardly know what to say to that. There is a difference between us."

"He doesn't seem like a Roman father - one who rules his family with a rod of iron."

"No; he is quite the reverse. He hasn't backbone enough."

"So it seemed to me when I saw him at the exhibition of the academy. You ought to be able to get along with a father like that, Carl."

"So I could but for one thing."

"What is that?"

"I have a stepmother!" said Carl, with a significant

glance at his companion.

"So have I, but she is the soul of kindness, and makes our home the dearest place in the world."

"Are there such stepmothers? I shouldn't have judged so from my own experience."

"I think I love her as much as if she were my own mother."

"You are lucky," said Carl, sighing.

"Tell me about yours."

"She was married to my father five years ago. Up to the time of her marriage I thought her amiable and sweet-tempered. But soon after the wedding she threw off the mask, and made it clear that she disliked me. One reason is that she has a son of her own about my age, a mean, sneaking fellow, who is the apple of her eye. She has been jealous of me, and tried to supplant me in the affection of my father, wishing Peter to be the favored son."

"How has she succeeded?"

"I don't think my father feels any love for Peter, but through my stepmother's influence he generally fares better than I do."

"Why wasn't he sent to school with you?"

"Because he is lazy and doesn't like study. Besides, his mother prefers to have him at home. During my absence she worked upon my father, by telling all sorts

Horatio Alger, Jr.

of malicious stories about me, till he became estranged from me, and little by little Peter has usurped my place as the favorite."

"Why didn't you deny the stories?" asked Gilbert.

"I did, but no credit was given to my denials. My step-mother was continually poisoning my father's mind against me."

"Did you give her cause? Did you behave disrespect-fully to her?"

"No," answered Carl, warmly. "I was prepared to give her a warm welcome, and treat her as a friend, but my advances were so coldly received that my heart was chilled."

"Poor Carl! How long has this been so?"

"From the beginning - ever since Mrs. Crawford came into the house."

"What are your relations with your step-brother - what's his name?"

"Peter Cook. I despise the boy, for he is mean, and tyrannical where he dares to be."

"I don't think it would be safe for him to bully you, Carl."

"He tried it, and got a good thrashing. You can imagine what followed. He ran, crying to his mother, and his version of the story was believed. I was confined to my room for a week, and forced to live on bread and water."

"I shouldn't think your father was a man to inflict such a punishment."

"It wasn't he - it was my stepmother. She insisted upon it, and he yielded. I heard afterwards from one of the servants that he wanted me released at the end of twenty-four hours, but she would not consent."

"How long ago was this?"

"It happened when I was twelve."

"Was it ever repeated?"

"Yes, a month later; but the punishment lasted only for two days."

"And you submitted to it?"

"I had to, but as soon as I was released I gave Peter such a flogging, with the promise to repeat it, if I was ever punished in that manner again, that the boy himself was panic-stricken, and objected to my being imprisoned again."

"He must be a charming fellow!"

"You would think so if you should see him. He has small, insignificant features, a turn-up nose, and an ugly scowl that appears whenever he is out of humor."

"And yet your father likes him?"

"I don't think he does, though Peter, by his mother's

Horatio Alger, Jr.

orders, pays all sorts of small attentions -bringing him his slippers, running on errands, and so on, not because he likes it, but because he wants to supplant me, as he has succeeded in doing."

"You have finally broken away, then?"

"Yes; I couldn't stand it any longer. Home had become intolerable."

"Pardon the question, but hasn't your father got considerable property?"

"I have every reason to think so."

"Won't your leaving home give your step-mother and Peter the inside track, and lead, perhaps, to your disinheritance?"

"I suppose so," answered Carl, wearily; "but no matter what happens, I can't bear to stay at home any longer."

"You're badly fixed - that's a fact!" said Gilbert, in a tone of sympathy. "What are your plans?"

"I don't know. I haven't had time to think."

CHAPTER II.

A FRIEND WORTH HAVING.

Gilbert wrinkled up his forehead and set about trying to form some plans for Carl.

"It will be hard for you to support yourself," he said, after a pause; "that is, without help."

"There is no one to help me. I expect no help."

"I thought your father might be induced to give you an allowance, so that with what you can earn, you may get along comfortably."

"I think father would be willing to do this, but my stepmother would prevent him."

"Then she has a great deal of influence over him?"

"Yes, she can twist him round her little finger."

"I can't understand it."

"You see, father is an invalid, and is very nervous. If he were in perfect health he would have more force of character and firmness. He is under the impression that he has heart disease, and it makes him timid

Horatio Alger, Jr.

and vacillating."

"Still he ought to do something for you."

"I suppose he ought. Still, Gilbert, I think I can earn my living."

"What can you do?"

"Well, I have a fair education. I could be an entry clerk, or a salesman in some store, or, if the worst came to the worst, I could work on a farm. I believe farmers give boys who work for them their board and clothes."

"I don't think the clothes would suit you."

"I am pretty well supplied with clothing."

Gilbert looked significantly at the gripsack.

"Do you carry it all in there?" he asked, doubtfully.

Carl laughed.

"Well, no," he answered. "I have a trunkful of clothes at home, though."

"Why didn't you bring them with you?"

"I would if I were an elephant. Being only a boy, I would find it burdensome carrying a trunk with me. The gripsack is all I can very well manage."

"I tell you what," said Gilbert. "Come round to our house and stay overnight. We live only a mile from here, you know. The folks will be glad to see you, and while you are there I will go to your house, see the governor, and arrange for an allowance for you that will make you comparatively independent."

"Thank you, Gilbert; but I don't feel like asking favors from those who have ill-treated me."

"Nor would I - of strangers; but Dr. Crawford is your father. It isn't right that Peter, your stepbrother, should be supported in ease and luxury, while you, the real son, should be subjected to privation and want."

"I don't know but you are right," admitted Carl, slowly.

"Of course I am right. Now, will you make me your minister plenipotentiary, armed with full powers?"

"Yes, I believe I will."

"That's right. That shows you are a boy of sense. Now, as you are subject to my directions, just get on that bicycle and I will carry your gripsack, and we will seek Vance Villa, as we call it when we want to be high-toned, by the most direct route."

"No, no, Gilbert; I will carry my own gripsack. I won't burden you with it," said Carl, rising from his recumbent position.

"Look here, Carl, how far have you walked with it this morning?"

"About twelve miles."

"Then, of course, you're tired, and require rest. Just

Horatio Alger, Jr.

jump on that bicycle, and I'll take the gripsack. If you have carried it twelve miles, I can surely carry it one."

"You are very kind, Gilbert."

"Why shouldn't I be?"

"But it is imposing up on your good nature."

But Gilbert had turned his head in a backward direction, and nodded in a satisfied way as he saw a light, open buggy rapidly approaching.

"There's my sister in that carriage," he said. "She comes in good time. I will put you and your gripsack in with her, and I'll take to my bicycle again."

"Your sister may not like such an arrangement."

"Won't she though! She's very fond of beaux, and she will receive you very graciously."

"You make me feel bashful, Gilbert."

"You won't be long. Julia will chat away to you as if she'd known you for fifty years."

"I was very young fifty years ago," said Carl, smiling.

"Hi, there, Jule!" called Gilbert, waving his hand.

Julia Vance stopped the horse, and looked inquiringly and rather admiringly at Carl, who was a boy of fine appearance.

"Let me introduce you to my friend and schoolmate,

Carl Crawford."

Carl took off his hat politely.

"I am very glad to make your acquaintance, Mr. Crawford," said Julia, demurely; "I have often heard Gilbert speak of you."

"I hope he said nothing bad about me, Miss Vance."

"You may be sure he didn't. If he should now - I wouldn't believe him."

"You've made a favorable impression, Carl," said Gilbert, smiling.

"I am naturally prejudiced against boys - having such a brother," said Julia; "but it is not fair to judge all boys by him."

"That is outrageous injustice!" said Gilbert; "but then, sisters seldom appreciate their brothers."

"Some other fellows' sisters may," said Carl.

"They do, they do!"

"Did you ever see such a vain, conceited boy, Mr. Crawford?"

"Of course you know him better than I do."

"Come, Carl; it's too bad for you, too, to join against me. However, I will forget and forgive. Jule, my friend, Carl, has accepted my invitation to make us a visit."

"I am very glad, I am sure," said Julia, sincerely.

"And I want you to take him in, bag and baggage, and convey him to our palace, while I speed thither on my wheel."

"To be sure I will, and with great pleasure."

"Can't you get out and assist him into the carriage, Jule?"

"Thank you," said Carl; "but though I am somewhat old and quite infirm, I think I can get in without troubling your sister. Are you sure, Miss Vance, you won't be incommoded by my gripsack?"

"Not at all."

"Then I will accept your kind offer."

In a trice Carl was seated next to Julia, with his valise at his feet.

"Won't you drive, Mr. Crawford?" said the young lady.

"Don't let me take the reins from you."

"I don't think it looks well for a lady to drive when a gentleman is sitting beside her."

Carl was glad to take the reins, for he liked driving.

"Now for a race!" said Gilbert, who was mounted on his bicycle.

"All right!" replied Carl. "Look out for us!"

They started, and the two kept neck and neck till they entered the driveway leading up to a handsome country mansion.

Carl followed them into the house, and was cordially received by Mr. and Mrs. Vance, who were very kind and hospitable, and were favorably impressed by the gentlemanly appearance of their son's friend.

Half an hour later dinner was announced, and Carl, having removed the stains of travel in his schoolmate's room, descended to the dining-room, and, it must be confessed, did ample justice to the bounteous repast spread before him.

In the afternoon Julia, Gilbert and he played tennis, and had a trial at archery. The hours glided away very rapidly, and six o'clock came before they were aware.

"Gilbert," said Carl, as they were preparing for tea, "you have a charming home."

"You have a nice house, too, Carl."

"True; but it isn't a home - to me. There is no love there."

"That makes a great difference."

"If I had a father and mother like yours I should be happy."

"You must stay here till day after tomorrow, and I will devote to-morrow to a visit in your interest to your home. I will beard the lion in his den - that is, your stepmother. Do you consent?"

"Yes, I consent; but it won't do any good."

"We will see."

CHAPTER III.

INTRODUCES PETER COOK.

Gilbert took the morning train to the town of Edgewood Center, the residence of the Crawfords. He had been there before, and knew that Carl's home was nearly a mile distant from the station. Though there was a hack in waiting, he preferred to walk, as it would give him a chance to think over what he proposed to say to Dr. Crawford in Carl's behalf.

He was within a quarter of a mile of his destination when his attention was drawn to a boy of about his own age, who was amusing himself and a smaller companion by firing stones at a cat that had taken refuge in a tree. Just as Gilbert came up, a stone took effect, and the poor cat moaned in affright, but did not dare to come down from her perch, as this would put her in the power of her assailant.

"That must be Carl's stepbrother, Peter," Gilbert decided, as he noted the boy's mean face and turn-up nose. "Stoning cats seems to be his idea of amusement. I shall take the liberty of interfering."

Peter Cook laughed heartily at his successful aim.

"I hit her, Simon," he said. "Doesn't she look seared?"

"You must have hurt her."

"I expect I did. I'll take a bigger stone next time."

He suited the action to the word, and picked up a rock which, should it hit the poor cat, would in all probability kill her, and prepared to fire.

"Put down that rock!" said Gilbert, indignantly.

Peter turned quickly, and eyed Gilbert insolently.

"Who are you?" he demanded.

"No matter who I am. Put down that rock!"

"What business is it of yours?"

"I shall make it my business to protect that cat from your cruelty."

Peter, who was a natural coward, took courage from having a companion to back him up, and retorted: "You'd better clear out of here, or I may fire at you."

"Do it if you dare!" said Gilbert, quietly.

Peter concluded that it would be wiser not to carry out his threat, but was resolved to keep to his original purpose. He raised his arm again, and took aim; but Gilbert rushed in, and striking his arm forcibly, compelled him to drop it.

"What do you mean by that, you loafer?" demanded Peter, his eyes blazing with anger.

"To stop your fun, if that's what you call it."

"I've a good mind to give you a thrashing."

Gilbert put himself in a position of defense.

"Sail in, if you want to!" he responded.

"Help me, Simon!" said Peter. "You grab his legs, and I'll upset him."

Simon, who, though younger, was braver than Peter, without hesitation followed directions. He threw himself on the ground and grasped Gilbert by the legs, while Peter, doubling up his fists, made a rush at his enemy. But Gilbert, swiftly eluding Simon, struck out with his right arm, and Peter, unprepared for so forcible a defense, tumbled over on his back, and Simon ran to his assistance.

Gilbert put himself on guard, expecting a second attack; but Peter apparently thought it wiser to fight with his tongue.

"You rascal!" he shrieked, almost foaming at the mouth; "I'll have you arrested."

"What for?" asked Gilbert, coolly.

"For flying at me like a - a tiger, and trying to kill me."

Gilbert laughed at this curious version of things.

"I thought it was you who flew at me," he said.

"What business had you to interfere with me?"

"I'll do it again unless you give up firing stones at the cat."

"I'll do it as long as I like."

"She's gone!" said Simon.

The boys looked up into the tree, and could see nothing of puss. She had taken the opportunity, when her assailant was otherwise occupied, to make good her escape.

"I'm glad of it!" said Gilbert. "Good-morning, boys! When we meet again, I hope you will be more creditably employed."

"You don't get off so easy, you loafer," said Peter, who saw the village constable approaching. "Here, Mr. Rogers, I want you to arrest this boy."

Constable Rogers, who was a stout, broad-shouldered man, nearly six feet in height, turned from one to the other, and asked: "What has he done?"

"He knocked me over. I want him arrested for assault and battery."

"And what did you do?"

"I? I didn't do anything."

"That is rather strange. Young man, what is your name?"

"Gilbert Vance."

"You don't live in this town?"

"No; I live in Warren."

"What made you attack Peter?"

"Because he flew at me, and I had to defend myself."

"Is this so, Simon? You saw all that happened."

"Ye - es," admitted Simon, unwillingly.

"That puts a different face on the matter. I don't see how I can arrest this boy. He had a right to defend himself."

"He came up and abused me - the loafer," said Peter.

"That was the reason you went at him?"

"Yes."

"Have you anything to say?" asked the constable, addressing Gilbert.

"Yes, sir; when I came up I saw this boy firing stones at a cat, who had taken refuge in that tree over there. He had just hit her, and had picked up a larger stone to fire when I ordered him to drop it."

"It was no business of yours," muttered Peter.

"I made it my business, and will again."

"Did the cat have a white spot on her forehead?" asked the constable.

"Yes, sir."

Horatio Alger, Jr.

"And was mouse colored?"

"Yes, sir."

"Why, it's my little girl's cat. She would be heartbroken if the cat were seriously hurt. You young rascal!" he continued, turning suddenly upon Peter, and shaking him vigorously. "Let me catch you at this business again, and I'll give you such a warming that you'll never want to touch another cat."

"Let me go!" cried the terrified boy. "I didn't know it was your cat."

"It would have been just as bad if it had been some-body else's cat. I ve a great mind to put you in the lockup."

"Oh, don't, please don't, Mr. Rogers!" implored Peter, quite panic-stricken.

"Will you promise never to stone another cat?"

"Yes, sir."

"Then go about your business."

Peter lost no time, but scuttled up the street with his companion.

"I am much obliged to you for protecting Flora's cat," then said the constable to Gilbert.

"You are quite welcome, sir. I won't see any animal abused if I can help it."

"You are right there."

"Wasn't that boy Peter Cook?"

"Yes. Don't you know him?"

"No; but I know his stepbrother, Carl."

"A different sort of boy! Have you come to visit him?"

"No; he is visiting me. In fact, he has left home, because he could not stand his step-mother's ill-treatment, and I have come to see his father in his behalf."

"He has had an uncomfortable home. Dr. Crawford is an invalid, and very much under the influence of his wife, who seems to have a spite against Carl, and is devoted to that young cub to whom you have given a lesson. Does Carl want to come back?"

"No; he wants to strike out for himself, but I told him it was no more than right that he should receive some help from his father."

"That is true enough. For nearly all the doctor's money came to him through Carl's mother."

"I am afraid Peter and his mother won't give me a very cordial welcome after what has happened this morning. I wish I could see the doctor alone."

"So you can, for there he is coming up the street."

Gilbert looked in the direction indicated, and his glance fell on a thin, fragile-looking man, evidently an invalid, with a weak, undecided face, who was slowly approaching.

The boy advanced to meet him, and, taking off his hat, asked politely: "Is this Dr. Crawford?"

CHAPTER IV.

AN IMPORTANT CONFERENCE.

Dr. Crawford stopped short, and eyed Gilbert attentively.

"I don't know you," he said, in a querulous tone.

"I am a schoolmate of your son, Carl. My name is Gilbert Vance."

"If you have come to see my son you will be disappointed. He has treated me in a shameful manner. He left home yesterday morning, and I don't know where he is."

"I can tell you, sir. He is staying - for a day or two - at my father's house."

"Where is that?" asked Dr. Crawford, his manner showing that he was confused.

"In Warren, thirteen miles from here."

"I know the town. What induced him to go to your house? Have you encouraged him to leave home?" inquired Dr. Crawford, with a look of displeasure.

"No, sir. It was only by chance that I met him a mile from our home. I induced him to stay overnight."

"Did you bring me any message from him?" "No, sir, except that he is going to strike out for himself, as he thinks his home an unhappy one."

"That is his own fault. He has had enough to eat and enough to wear. He has had as comfortable a home as yourself."

"I don't doubt that, but he complains that his stepmother is continually finding fault with him, and scolding him."

"He provokes her to do it. He is a headstrong, obstinate boy."

"He never had that reputation at school, sir. We all liked him."

"I suppose you mean to imply that I am in fault?" said the doctor, warmly.

"I don't think you know how badly Mrs. Crawford treats Carl, sir."

"Of course, of course. That is always said of a stepmother."

"Not always, sir. I have a stepmother myself, and no own mother could treat me better."

"You are probably a better boy."

"I can't accept the compliment. I hope you'll excuse me

saying it, Dr. Crawford, but if my stepmother treated me as Carl says Mrs. Crawford treats him I wouldn't stay in the house another day."

"Really, this is very annoying," said Dr. Crawford, irritably. "Have you come here from Warren to say this?"

"No, sir, not entirely."

"Perhaps Carl wants me to receive him back. I will do so if he promises to obey his stepmother."

"That he won't do, I am sure."

"Then what is the object of your visit?"

"To say that Carl wants and intends to earn his own living. But it is hard for a boy of his age, who has never worked, to earn enough at first to pay for his board and clothes. He asks, or, rather, I ask for him, that you will allow him a small sum, say three or four dollars a week, which is considerably less than he must cost you at home, for a time until he gets on his feet."

"I don't know," said Dr. Crawford, in a vacillating tone. "I don't think Mrs. Crawford would approve this."

"It seems to me you are the one to decide, as Carl is your own son. Peter must cost you a good deal more."

"Do you know Peter?"

"I have met him," answered Gilbert, with a slight smile.

"I don't know what to say. You may be right. Peter does cost me more."

"And Carl is entitled to be treated as well as he."

"I think I ought to speak to Mrs. Crawford about it. And, by the way, I nearly forgot to say that she charges Carl with taking money from her bureau drawer before he went away. It was a large sum, too - twenty-five dollars."

"That is false!" exclaimed Gilbert, indignantly. "I am surprised that you should believe such a thing of your own son."

"Mrs. Crawford says she has proof," said the doctor, hesitating.

"Then what has he done with the money? I know that he has but thirty-seven cents with him at this time, and he only left home yesterday. If the money has really been taken, I think I know who took it."

"Who?"

"Peter Cook. He looks mean enough for anything."

"What right have you to speak so of Peter?"

"Because I caught him stoning a cat this morning. He would have killed the poor thing if I had not interfered. I consider that worse than taking money."

"I - I don't know what to say. I can't agree to anything till I have spoken with Mrs. Crawford. Did you say that Carl had but thirty seven cents?"

"Yes, sir; I presume you don't want him to starve?"

"No, of course not. He is my son, though he has behaved badly. Here, give him that!" and Dr. Crawford drew a ten-dollar bill from his wallet, and handed it to Gilbert

"Thank you, sir. This money will be very useful. Besides, it will show Carl that his father is not wholly indifferent to him."

"Of course not. Who says that I am a bad father?" asked Dr. Crawford, peevishly.

"I don't think, sir, there would be any difficulty between you and Carl if you had not married again."

"Carl has no right to vex Mrs. Crawford. Besides, he can't agree with Peter."

"Is that his fault or Peter's?" asked Gilbert, significantly.

"I am not acquainted with the circumstances, but Mrs. Crawford says that Carl is always bullying Peter."

"He never bullied anyone at school."

"Is there anything, else you want?"

"Yes, sir; Carl only took away a little underclothing in a gripsack. He would like his woolen clothes put in his trunk, and to have it sent -"

"Where?"

"Perhaps it had better be sent to my house. There are one or two things in his room also that he asked me to get."

"Why didn't he come himself?"

"Because he thought it would be unpleasant for him to meet Mrs. Crawford. They would be sure to quarrel."

"Well, perhaps he is right," said Dr. Crawford, with an air of relief. "About the allowance, I shall have to consult my wife. Will you come with me to the house?"

"Yes, sir; I should like to have the matter settled to-day, so that Carl will know what to depend upon."

Gilbert rather dreaded the interview he was likely to have with Mrs. Crawford; but he was acting for Carl, and his feelings of friendship were strong.

So he walked beside Dr. Crawford till they reached the tasteful dwelling occupied as a residence by Carl and his father.

"How happy Carl could he here, if he had a stepmother like mine," Gilbert thought.

They went up to the front door, which was opened for them by a servant.

"Jane, is Mrs. Crawford in?" asked the doctor.

"No, sir; not just now. She went to the village to do some shopping."

"Is Peter in?"

"No, sir."

"Then you will have to wait till they return."

"Can't I go up to Carl's room and be packing his things?"

"Yes, I think you may. I don't think Mrs. Crawford would object."

"Good heavens! Hasn't the man a mind of his own?" thought Gilbert.

"Jane, you may show this young gentleman up to Master Carl's room, and give him the key of his trunk. He is going to pack his clothes."

"When is Master Carl coming back?" asked Jane.

"I - I don't know. I think he will be away for a time."

"I wish it was Peter instead of him," said Jane, in a low voice, only audible to Gilbert.

She showed Gilbert the way upstairs, while the doctor went to his study.

"Are you a friend of Master Carl's?" asked Jane, as soon as they were alone.

"Yes, Jane."

"And where is he?"

"At my house."

"Is he goin' to stay there?"

"For a short time. He wants to go out into the world and make his own living."

"And no wonder - poor boy! It's hard times he had here."

"Didn't Mrs. Crawford treat him well?" asked Gilbert, with curiosity

"Is it trate him well? She was a-jawin' an' a-jawin' him from mornin' till night. Ugh, but she's an ugly cr'atur'!"

"How about Peter?"

"He's just as bad - the m'anest bye I iver set eyes on. It would do me good to see him flogged."

She chatted a little longer with Gilbert, helping him to find Carl's clothes, when suddenly a shrill voice was heard calling her from below.

"Shure, it's the madam!" said Jane, shrugging her shoulders. "I expect she's in a temper;" and she rose from her knees and hurried downstairs.

CHAPTER V.

CARL'S STEPMOTHER.

Five minutes later, as Gilbert was closing the trunk, Jane reappeared.

"The doctor and Mrs. Crawford would like to see you downstairs," she said.

Gilbert followed Jane into the library, where Dr. Crawford and his wife were seated. He looked with interest at the woman who had made home so disagreeable to Carl, and was instantly prejudiced against her. She was light complexioned, with very light-brown hair, cold, gray eyes, and a disagreeable expression which seemed natural to her.

"My dear," said the doctor, "this is the young man who has come from Carl."

Mrs. Crawford surveyed Gilbert with an expression by no means friendly.

"What is your name?" she asked.

"Gilbert Vance."

"Did Carl Crawford send you here?"

"No; I volunteered to come."

"Did he tell you that he was disobedient and disrespectful to me?"

"No; he told me that you treated him so badly that he was unwilling to live in the same house with you," answered Gilbert, boldly.

"Well, upon my word!" exclaimed Mrs. Crawford, fanning herself vigorously. "Dr. Crawford, did you hear that?"

"Yes."

"And what do you think of it?"

"Well, I think you may have been too hard upon Carl."

"Too hard? Why, then, did he not treat me respectfully? This boy seems inclined to be impertinent."

"I answered your questions, madam," said Gilbert, coldly.

"I suppose you side with your friend Carl?"

"I certainly do."

Mrs. Crawford bit her lip.

"What is the object of your coming? Does Carl wish to return?"

"I thought Dr. Crawford might have told you."

"Carl wants his clothes sent to him," said the doctor. "He only carried a few with him."

"I shall not consent to it. He deserves no favors at our hands."

This was too much even for Dr. Crawford.

"You go too far, Mrs. Crawford," he said. "I am sensible of the boy's faults, but I certainly will not allow his clothes to be withheld from him."

"Oh, well! spoil him if you choose!" said the lady, sullenly. "Take his part against your wife!"

"I have never done that, but I will not allow him to be defrauded of his clothes."

"I have no more to say," said Mrs. Crawford, her eyes snapping. She was clearly mortified at her failure to carry her point.

"Do you wish the trunk to be sent to your house?" asked the doctor.

"Yes, sir; I have packed the clothes and locked the trunk."

"I should like to examine it before it goes," put in Mrs. Crawford, spitefully.

"Why?"

"To make sure that nothing has been put in that does not belong to Carl."

Horatio Alger, Jr.

"Do you mean to accuse me of stealing, madam?" demanded Gilbert, indignantly.

Mrs. Crawford tossed her head.

"I don't know anything about you," she replied.

"Dr. Crawford, am I to open the trunk?" asked Gilbert.

"No," answered the doctor, with unwonted decision.

"I hate that boy! He has twice subjected me to mortification," thought Mrs. Crawford.

"You know very well," she said, turning to her husband, "that I have grounds for my request. I blush to mention it, but I have reason to believe that your son took a wallet containing twenty-five dollars from my bureau drawer."

"I deny it!" said Gilbert.

"What do you know about it, I should like to ask?" sneered Mrs. Crawford.

"I know that Carl is an honorable boy, incapable of theft, and at this moment has but thirty-seven cents in his possession."

"So far as you know."

"If the money has really disappeared, madam, you had better ask your own boy about it."

"This is insufferable!" exclaimed Mrs. Crawford, her light eyes emitting angry flashes. "Who dares to say that Peter took the wallet?" she went on, rising to her feet.

There was an unexpected reply. Jane entered the room at this moment to ask a question.

"I say so, ma'am," she rejoined.

"What?" ejaculated Mrs. Crawford, with startling emphasis.

"I didn't mean to say anything about it till I found you were charging it on Master Carl. I saw Peter open your bureau drawer, take out the wallet, and put it in his pocket."

"It's a lie!" said Mrs. Crawford, hoarsely.

"It's the truth, though I suppose you don't want to believe it. If you want to know what he did with the money ask him how much he paid for the gold ring he bought of the jeweler down at the village."

"You are a spy - a base, dishonorable spy!" cried Mrs. Crawford.

"I won't say what you are, ma'am, to bring false charges against Master Carl, and I wonder the doctor will believe them."

"Leave the house directly, you hussy!" shrieked Mrs. Crawford.

"If I do, I wonder who'll get the dinner?" remarked Jane, not at all disturbed.

Horatio Alger, Jr.

"I won't stay here to be insulted," said the angry lady. "Dr. Crawford, you might have spirit enough to defend your wife."

She flounced out of the room, not waiting for a reply, leaving the doctor dazed and flurried.

"I hope, sir, you are convinced now that Carl did not take Mrs. Crawford's money," said Gilbert. "I told you it was probably Peter."

"Are you sure of what you said, Jane?" asked the doctor.

"Yes, sir. I saw Peter take the wallet with my own eyes."

"It is his mother's money, and they must settle it between them I am glad Carl did not take it. Really, this has been a very unpleasant scene."

"I am sorry for my part in it. Carl is my friend, and I feel that I ought to stand up for his rights," remarked Gilbert.

"Certainly, certainly, that is right. But you see how I am placed."

"I see that this is no place for Carl. If you will allow me, I will send an expressman for the trunk, and take it with me to the station."

"Yes, I see no objection. I - I would invite you to dinner, but Mrs. Crawford seems to be suffering from a nervous attack, and it might not be pleasant."

"I agree with you, sir."

Just then Peter entered the room, and looked at Gilbert with surprise and wrath, remembering his recent discomfiture at the hands of the young visitor.

"My stepson, Peter," announced Dr. Crawford.

"Peter and I have met before," said Gilbert, smiling.

"What are you here for?" asked Peter, rudely.

"Not to see you," answered Gilbert, turning from him.

"My mother'll have something to say to you," went on Peter, significantly.

"She will have something to say to you," retorted Gilbert. "She has found out who stole her money."

Peter's face turned scarlet instantly, and he left the room hurriedly.

"Perhaps I ought not to have said that, Dr. Crawford," added Gilbert, apologetically, "but I dislike that boy very much, and couldn't help giving him as good as he sent."

"It is all very unpleasant," responded Dr. Crawford, peevishly. "I don't see why I can't live in peace and tranquility."

"I won't intrude upon you any longer," said Gilbert, "if you will kindly tell me whether you will consent to make Carl a small weekly allowance."

"I can't say now. I want time to think. Give me your address, and I will write to Carl in your care."

"Very well, sir."

Gilbert left the house and made arrangements to have Carl's trunk called for. It accompanied him on the next train to Warren.

CHAPTER VI.

Mrs. CRAWFORD'S LETTER.

"How did you like my stepmother?" asked Carl, when Gilbert returned in the afternoon.

"She's a daisy!" answered Gilbert, shrugging his shoulders. "I don't think I ever saw a more disagreeable woman."

"Do you blame me for leaving home?"

"I only wonder you have been able to stay so long. I had a long conversation with your father."

"Mrs. Crawford has made a different man of him. I should have no trouble in getting along with him if there was no one to come between us."

"He gave me this for you," said Gilbert, producing the ten-dollar bill.

"Did my stepmother know of his sending it?"

"No; she was opposed to sending your trunk, but your father said emphatically you should have it."

"I am glad he showed that much spirit."

"I have some hopes that he will make you an allowance of a few dollars a week."

"That would make me all right, but I don't expect it."

"You will probably hear from your father to-morrow or next day, so you will have to make yourself contented a little longer."

"I hope you are not very homesick, Mr. Crawford?" said Julia, coquettishly.

"I would ask nothing better than to stay here permanently," rejoined Carl, earnestly. "This is a real home. I have met with more kindness here than in six months at my own home."

"You have one staunch friend at home," said Gilbert.

"You don't allude to Peter?"

"So far as I can judge, he hates you like poison. I mean Jane."

"Yes, Jane is a real friend. She has been in the family for ten years. She was a favorite with my own mother, and feels an interest in me."

"By the way, your stepmother's charge that you took a wallet containing money from her drawer has been disproved by Jane. She saw Peter abstracting the money, and so informed Mrs. Crawford."

"I am not at all surprised. Peter is mean enough to steal or do anything else. What did my stepmother say?"

"She was very angry, and threatened to discharge Jane; but, as no one would be left to attend to the dinner, I presume she is likely to stay."

"I ought to be forming some plan," said Carl, thoughtfully.

"Wait till you hear from home. Julia will see that your time is well filled up till then. Dismiss all care, and enjoy yourself while you may."

This seemed to be sensible advice, and Carl followed it. In the evening some young people were invited in, and there was a round of amusements that made Carl forget that he was an exile from home, with very dubious prospects.

"You are all spoiling me," he said, as Gilbert and he went upstairs to bed. "I am beginning to understand the charms of home. To go out into the world from here will be like taking a cold shower bath."

"Never forget, Carl, that you will be welcome back, whenever you feel like coming," said Gilbert, laying his band affectionately on Carl's shoulder. "We all like you here."

"Thank you, old fellow! I appreciate the kindness I have received here; but I must strike out for myself."

"How do you feel about it, Carl?"

"I hope for the best. I am young, strong and willing to work. There must be an opening for me somewhere."

The next morning, just after breakfast, a letter arrived

Horatio Alger, Jr.

for Carl, mailed at Edgewood Center.

"Is it from your father?" asked Gilbert.

"No; it is in the handwriting of my stepmother. I can guess from that that it contains no good news."

He opened the letter, and as he read it his face expressed disgust and annoyance.

"Read it, Gilbert," he said, handing him the open sheet.

This was the missive:

"CARL CRAWFORD: - AS your father has a nervous attack, brought on by your misconduct, he has authorized me to write to you. As you are but sixteen, he could send for you and have you forcibly brought back, but deems it better for you to follow your own course and suffer the punishment of your obstinate and perverse conduct. The boy whom you sent here proved a fitting messenger. He seems, if possible, to be even worse than yourself. He was very impertinent to me, and made a brutal and unprovoked attack on my poor boy, Peter, whose devotion to your father and myself forms an agreeable contrast to your studied disregard of our wishes.

"Your friend had the assurance to ask for a weekly allowance for you while a voluntary exile from the home where you have been only too well treated. In other words, you want to be paid for your disobedience. Even if your father were weak enough to think of complying with this extraordinary request, I should do my best to dissuade him."

"Small doubt of that!" said Carl, bitterly.

"In my sorrow for your waywardness, I am comforted by the thought that Peter is too good and conscientious ever to follow your example. While you are away, he will do his utmost to make up to your father for his disappointment in you. That you may grow wise in time, and turn at length from the error of your ways, is the earnest hope of your stepmother,

Anastasia Crawford."

"It makes me sick to read such a letter as that, Gilbert," said Carl. "And to have that sneak and thief - as he turned out to be - Peter, set up as a model for me, is a little too much."

"I never knew there were such women in the world!" returned Gilbert. "I can understand your feelings perfectly, after my interview of yesterday."

"She thinks even worse of you than of me," said Carl, with a faint smile.

"I have no doubt Peter shares her sentiments. I didn't make many friends in your family, it must be confessed."

"You did me a service, Gilbert, and I shall not soon forget it."

"Where did your stepmother come from?" asked

Gilbert, thoughtfully.

"I don't know. My father met her at some summer resort. She was staying in the same boarding house, she and the angelic Peter. She lost no time in setting her cap for my father, who was doubtless reported to her as a man of property, and she succeeded in capturing him."

"I wonder at that. She doesn't seem very fascinating."

"She made herself very agreeable to my father, and was even affectionate in her manner to me, though I couldn't get to like her. The end was that she became Mrs. Crawford. Once installed in our house, she soon threw off the mask and showed herself in her true colors, a cold-hearted, selfish and disagreeable woman."

"I wonder your father doesn't recognize her for what she is."

"She is very artful, and is politic enough to treat him well. She has lost no opportunity of prejudicing him against me. If he were not an invalid she would find her task more difficult."

"Did she have any property when your father married her?"

"Not that I have been able to discover. She is scheming to have my father leave the lion's share of his property to her and Peter. I dare say she will succeed."

"Let us hope your father will live till you are a young man, at least, and better able to cope with her."

"I earnestly hope so."

"Your father is not an old man."

"He is fifty-one, but he is not strong. I believe he has liver complaint. At any rate, I know that when, at my stepmother's instigation, he applied to an insurance company to insure his life for her benefit, the application was rejected."

"You don't know anything of Mrs. Crawford's antecedents?"

"No."

"What was her name before she married your father?"

"She was a Mrs. Cook. That, as you know, is Peter's name."

"Perhaps, in your travels, you may learn something of her history."

"I should like to do so."

"You won't leave us to-morrow?"

"I must go to-day. I know now that I must depend wholly upon my own exertions, and I must get to work as soon as possible."

"You will write to me, Carl?"

"Yes, when I have anything agreeable to write."

"Let us hope that will be soon."

CHAPTER VII.

ENDS IN A TRAGEDY.

Carl obtained permission to leave his trunk at the Vance mansion, merely taking out what he absolutely needed for a change.

"When I am settled I will send for it," he said. "Now I shouldn't know what to do with it."

There were cordial good-bys, and Carl started once more on the tramp. He might, indeed, have traveled by rail, for he had ten dollars and thirty-seven cents; but it occurred to him that in walking he might meet with some one who would give him employment. Besides, he was not in a hurry to get on, nor had he any definite destination. The day was fine, there was a light breeze, and he experienced a hopeful exhilaration as he walked lightly on, with the world before him, and any number of possibilities in the way of fortunate adventures that might befall him.

He had walked five miles, when, to the left, he saw an elderly man hard at work in a hay field. He was leaning on his rake, and looking perplexed and troubled. Carl paused to rest, and as he looked over the rail fence, attracted the attention of the farmer.

"I say, young feller, where are you goin'?" he asked.

"I don't know - exactly."

"You don't know where you are goin'?" repeated the farmer, in surprise.

Carl laughed. "I am going out in the world to seek my fortune," he said.

"You be? Would you like a job?" asked the farmer, eagerly.

"What sort of a job?"

"I'd like to have you help me hayin'. My hired man is sick, and he's left me in a hole. It's goin' to rain, and -"

"Going to rain?" repeated Carl, in surprise, as he looked up at the nearly cloudless sky.

"Yes. It don't look like it, I know, but old Job Hagar say it'll rain before night, and what he don't know about the weather ain't worth knowin'. I want to get the hay on this meadow into the barn, and then I'll feel safe, rain or shine."

"And you want me to help you?"

"Yes; you look strong and hardy."

"Yes, I am pretty strong," said Carl, complacently.

"Well, what do you say?"

"All right. I'll help you."

Horatio Alger, Jr.

Carl gave a spring and cleared the fence, landing in the hay field, having first thrown his valise over.

"You're pretty spry," said the farmer. "I couldn't do that."

"No, you're too heavy," said Carl, smiling, as he noted the clumsy figure of his employer. "Now, what shall I do?"

"Take that rake and rake up the hay. Then we'll go over to the barn and get the hay wagon."

"Where is your barn?"

The farmer pointed across the fields to a story-and-a-half farmhouse, and standing near it a good-sized barn, brown from want of paint and exposure to sun and rain. The buildings were perhaps twenty-five rods distant.

"Are you used to hayin'?" asked the farmer.

"Well, no, not exactly; though I've handled a rake before."

Carl's experience, however, had been very limited. He had, to be sure, had a rake in his hand, but probably he had not worked more than ten minutes at it. However, raking is easily learned, and his want of experience was not detected. He started off with great enthusiasm, but after a while thought it best to adopt the more leisurely movements of the farmer. After two hours his hands began to blister, but still he kept on.

"I have got to make my living by hard work," he said

to himself, "and it won't do to let such a little thing as a blister interfere."

When he had been working a couple of hours, he began to feel hungry. His walk, and the work he had been doing, sharpened his appetite till he really felt uncomfortable. It was at this time - just twelve o'clock - that the farmer's wife came to the front door and blew a fish horn so vigorously that it could probably have been heard half a mile.

"The old woman's got dinner ready," said the farmer. "If you don't mind takin' your pay in victuals, you can go along home with me, and take a bite."

"I think I could take two or three, sir."

"Ho, ho! that's a good joke! Money's scarce, and I'd rather pay in victuals, if it's all the same to you."

"Do you generally find people willing to work for their board?" asked Carl, who knew that he was being imposed upon.

"Well, I might pay a leetle more. You work for me till sundown, and I'll give you dinner and supper, and - fifteen cents."

Carl wanted to laugh. At this rate of compensation he felt that it would take a long time to make a fortune, but he was so hungry that he would have accepted board alone if it had been necessary.

"I agree," he said. "Shall I leave my rake here?"

"Yes; it'll be all right."

"I'll take along my valise, for I can't afford to run any risk of losing it."

"Jest as you say."

Five minutes brought them to the farmhouse.

"Can I wash my hands?" asked Carl.

"Yes, you can go right to the sink and wash in the tin basin. There's a roll towel behind the door. Mis' Perkins" - that was the way he addressed his wife - "this is a young chap that I've hired to help me hayin'. You can set a chair for him at the table."

"All right, Silas. He don't look very old, though."

"No, ma'am. I ain't twenty-one yet," answered Carl, who was really sixteen.

"I shouldn't say you was. You ain't no signs of a mustache."

"I keep it short, ma'am, in warm weather," said Carl.

"It don't dull a razor any to cut it in cold weather, does it?" asked the farmer, chuckling at his joke.

"Well, no, sir; I can't say it does."

It was a boiled dinner that the farmer's wife provided, corned beef and vegetables, but the plebeian meal seemed to Carl the best he ever ate. Afterwards there was apple pudding, to which he did equal justice.

"I never knew work improved a fellow's appetite so,"

reflected the young traveler. "I never ate with so much relish at home."

After dinner they went back to the field and worked till the supper hour, five o'clock. By that time all the hay had been put into the barn.

"We've done a good day's work," said the farmer, in a tone of satisfaction, "and only just in time. Do you see that dark cloud?"

"Yes, sir."

"In half an hour there'll be rain, or I'm mistaken. Old Job Hagar is right after all."

The farmer proved a true prophet. In half an hour, while they were at the supper table, the rain began to come down in large drops - forming pools in the hollows of the ground, and drenching all exposed objects with the largesse of the heavens.

"Where war you a-goin' to-night?" asked the farmer.

"I don't know, sir."

"I was thinkin' that I'd give you a night's lodgin' in place of the fifteen cents I agreed to pay you. Money's very skeerce with me, and will be till I've sold off some of the crops."

"I shall be glad to make that arrangement," said Carl, who had been considering how much the farmer would ask for lodging, for there seemed small chance of continuing his journey. Fifteen cents was a lower price than he had calculated on.

"That's a sensible idea!" said the farmer, rubbing his hands with satisfaction at the thought that he had secured valuable help at no money outlay whatever.

The next morning Carl continued his tramp, refusing the offer of continued employment on the same terms. He was bent on pursuing his journey, though he did not know exactly where he would fetch up in the end.

At twelve o'clock that day he found himself in the outskirts of a town, with the same uncomfortable appetite that he had felt the day before, but with no hotel or restaurant anywhere near. There was, however, a small house, the outer door of which stood conveniently open. Through the open window, Carl saw a table spread as if for dinner, and he thought it probable that he could arrange to become a boarder for a single meal. He knocked at the door, but no one came. He shouted out: "Is anybody at home?" and received no answer. He went to a small barn just outside and peered in, but no one was to be seen.

What should he do? He was terribly hungry, and the sight of the food on the table was tantalizing.

"I'll go in, as the door is open," he decided, "and sit down to the table and eat. Somebody will be along before I get through, and I'll pay whatever is satisfactory, for eat I must."

He entered, seated himself, and ate heartily. Still no one appeared.

"I don't want to go off without paying," thought Carl. "I'll see if I can find somebody."

He opened the door into the kitchen, but it was deserted. Then he opened that of a small bedroom, and started back in terror and dismay.

There suspended from a hook - a man of middle age was hanging, with his head bent forward, his eyes wide open, and his tongue protruding from his mouth!

Horatio Alger, Jr.

CHAPTER VIII.

CARL FALLS UNDER SUSPICION.

To a person of any age such a sight as that described at the close of the last chapter might well have proved startling. To a boy like Carl it was simply overwhelming. It so happened that he had but twice seen a dead person, and never a victim of violence. The peculiar circumstances increased the effect upon his mind.

He placed his hand upon the man's face, and found that he was still warm. He could have been dead but a short time.

"What shall I do?" thought Carl, perplexed. "This is terrible!"

Then it flashed upon him that as he was alone with the dead man suspicion might fall upon him as being concerned in what night be called a murder.

"I had better leave here at once," he reflected. "I shall have to go away without paying for my meal."

He started to leave the house, but had scarcely reached the door when two persons - a man and a woman - entered. Both looked at Carl with suspicion.

"What are you doing here?" asked the man.

"I beg your pardon," answered Carl; "I was very hungry, and seeing no one about, took the liberty to sit down at the table and eat. I am willing to pay for my dinner if you will tell me how much it amounts to."

"Wasn't my husband here?" asked the woman.

"I - I am afraid something has happened to your husband," faltered Carl.

"What do you mean?"

Carl silently pointed to the chamber door. The woman opened it, and uttered a loud shriek.

"Look here, Walter!" she cried.

Her companion quickly came to her side.

"My husband is dead!" cried the woman; "basely murdered, and there," pointing fiercely to Carl, "there stands the murderer!"

"Madam, you cannot believe this!" said Carl, naturally agitated.

"What have you to say for yourself?" demanded the man, suspiciously.

"I only just saw - your husband," continued Carl, addressing himself to the woman. "I had finished my meal, when I began to search for some one whom I could pay, and so opened this door into the room beyond, when I saw - him hanging there!"

"Don't believe him, the red-handed murderer!" broke out the woman, fiercely. "He is probably a thief; he killed my poor husband, and then sat down like a cold-blooded villain that he is, and gorged himself."

Things began to look very serious for poor Carl.

"Your husband is larger and stronger than myself," he urged, desperately. "How could I overpower him?"

"It looks reasonable, Maria," said the man. "I don't see how the boy could have killed Mr. Brown, or lifted him upon the hook, even if he did not resist."

"He murdered him, I tell you, he murdered him!" shrieked the woman, who seemed bereft of reason. "I call upon you to arrest him."

"I am not a constable, Maria."

"Then tie him so he cannot get away, and go for a constable. I wouldn't feel safe with him in the house, unless he were tied fast. He might hang me!"

Terrible as the circumstances were, Carl felt an impulse to laugh. It seemed absurd to hear himself talked of in this way.

"Tie me if you like!" he said. "I am willing to wait here till some one comes who has a little common sense. Just remember that I am only a boy, and haven't the strength of a full-grown man!"

"The boy is right, Maria! It's a foolish idea of yours."

"I call upon you to tie the villain!" insisted the woman.

"Just as you say! Can you give me some rope?"

From a drawer Mrs. Brown drew a quantity of strong cord, and the man proceeded to tie Carl's hands.

"Tie his feet, too, Walter!"

"Even if you didn't tie me, I would promise to remain here. I don't want anybody to suspect me of such a thing," put in Carl.

"How artful he is!" said Mrs. Brown. "Tie him strong, Walter."

The two were left alone, Carl feeling decidedly uncomfortable. The newly-made widow laid her head upon the table and moaned, glancing occasionally at the body of her husband, as it still hung suspended from the hook.

"Oh, William, I little expected to find you dead!" she groaned. "I only went to the store to buy a pound of salt, and when I come back, I find you cold and still, the victim of a young ruffian! How could you be so wicked?" she demanded fiercely of Carl.

"I have told you that I had nothing to do with your husband's death, madam."

"Who killed him, then?" she cried.

"I don't know. He must have committed suicide."

"Don't think you are going to escape in that way. I won't rest till I see you hung!"

"I wish I had never entered the house," thought Carl, uncomfortably. "I would rather have gone hungry for twenty four hours longer than find myself in such a position."

Half an hour passed. Then a sound of voices was heard outside, and half a dozen men entered, including besides the messenger, the constable and a physician.

"Why was he not cut down?" asked the doctor, hastily. "There might have been a chance to resuscitate him."

"I didn't think of it," said the messenger. "Maria was so excited, and insisted that the boy murdered him."

"What boy?"

Carl was pointed out.

"That boy? What nonsense!" exclaimed Dr. Park. "Why, it would be more than you or I could do to overpower and hang a man weighing one hundred and seventy-five pounds."

"That's what I thought, but Maria seemed crazed like."

"I tell you he did it! Are you going to let him go, the red-handed murderer?"

"Loose the cord, and I will question the boy," said Dr. Park, with an air of authority.

Carl breathed a sigh of relief, when, freed from his bonds, he stood upright.

"I'll tell you all I know," he said, "but it won't throw

any light upon the death."

Dr. Park listened attentively, and asked one or two questions.

"Did you hear any noise when you were sitting at the table?" he inquired.

"No, sir."

"Was the door closed?"

"Yes, sir."

"That of itself would probably prevent your hearing anything. Mrs. Brown, at what hour did you leave the house?"

"At ten minutes of twelve."

"It is now five minutes of one. The deed must have been committed just after you left the house. Had you noticed anything out of the way in your - husband's manner?"

"No, sir, not much. He was always a silent man."

"Had anything happened to disturb him?"

"He got a letter this morning. I don't know what was in it."

"We had better search for it."

The body was taken down and laid on the bed. Dr. Park searched the pockets, and found a half sheet of note paper, on which these lines were written:

"Maria: - I have made up my mind I can live no longer. I have made a terrible discovery. When I married you, I thought my first wife, who deserted me four years ago, dead. I learn by a letter received this morning that she is still living in a town of Illinois. The only thing I can do is to free you both from my presence. When you come back from the store you will find me cold and dead. The little that I leave behind I give to you. If my first wife should come here, as she threatens, you can tell her so. Good-by.

"William."

The reading of this letter made a sensation. Mrs. Brown went into hysterics, and there was a scene of confusion.

"Do you think I can go?" Carl asked Dr. Park.

"Yes. There is nothing to connect you with the sad event."

Carl gladly left the cottage, and it was only when he was a mile on his way that he remembered that he had not paid for his dinner, after all.

CHAPTER IX.

A PLAUSIBLE STRANGER.

Three days later found Carl still on his travels. It was his custom to obtain his meals at a cheap hotel, or, if none were met with, at a farmhouse, and to secure lodgings where he could, and on as favorable terms as possible. He realized the need of economy, and felt that he was practicing it. He had changed his ten-dollar bill the first day, for a five and several ones. These last were now spent, and the five-dollar bill alone remained to him. He had earned nothing, though everywhere he had been on the lookout for a job.

Toward the close of the last day he overtook a young man of twenty-five, who was traveling in the same direction.

"Good-afternoon," said the young man, sociably.

"Good-afternoon, sir."

"Where are you bound, may I ask?"

"To the next town."

"Fillmore?"

"Yes, if that is the name."

"So am I. Why shouldn't we travel together?"

"I have no objection," said Carl, who was glad of company.

"Are you in any business?"

"No, but I hope to find a place."

"Oh, a smart boy like you will soon find employment."

"I hope so, I am sure. I haven't much money left, and it is necessary I should do something."

"Just so. I am a New York salesman, but just now I am on my vacation - taking a pedestrian tour with knapsack and staff, as you see. The beauty of it is that my salary runs on just as if I were at my post, and will nearly pay all my traveling expenses."

"You are in luck. Besides you have a good place to go back to. There isn't any vacancy, is there? You couldn't take on a boy?" asked Carl, eagerly.

"Well, there might be a chance," said the young man, slowly. "You haven't any recommendations with you, have you?"

"No; I have never been employed."

"It doesn't matter. I will recommend you myself."

"You might be deceived in me," said Carl, smiling.

"I'll take the risk of that. I know a reliable boy when I see him."

"Thank you. What is the name of your firm?"

"F. Brandes & Co., commission merchants, Pearl Street. My own name is Chauncy Hubbard, at your service."

"I am Carl Crawford."

"That's a good name. I predict that we shall be great chums, if I manage to get you a place in our establishment."

"Is Mr. Brandes a good man to work for?"

"Yes, he is easy and good-natured. He is liberal to his clerks. What salary do you think I get?"

"I couldn't guess."

"Forty dollars a week, and I am only twenty-five. Went into the house at sixteen, and worked my way up."

"You have certainly done well," said Carl, respectfully.

"Well, I'm no slouch, if I do say it myself."

"I don't wonder your income pays the expenses of your vacation trip."

"It ought to, that's a fact, though I'm rather free handed and like to spend money. My prospects are pretty good in another direction. Old Fred Brandes has a handsome daughter, who thinks considerable of your humble servant."

"Do you think there is any chance of marrying her?" asked Carl, with interest.

"I think my chance is pretty good, as the girl won't look at anybody else."

"Is Mr. Brandes wealthy?"

"Yes, the old man's pretty well fixed, worth nearly half a million, I guess."

"Perhaps he will take you into the firm," suggested Carl.

"Very likely. That's what I'm working for."

"At any rate, you ought to save something out of your salary."

"I ought, but I haven't. The fact is, Carl," said Chauncy Hubbard, in a burst of confidence, I have a great mind to make a confession to you."

"I shall feel flattered, I am sure," said Carl, politely.

"I have one great fault - I gamble."

"Do you?" said Carl, rather startled, for he had been brought up very properly to have a horror of gambling.

"Yes, I suppose it's in my blood. My father was a very rich man at one time, but he lost nearly all his fortune at the gaming table."

"That ought to have been a warning to you, I should think."

"It ought, and may be yet, for I am still a young man."

"Mr. Hubbard," said Carl, earnestly, "I feel rather diffident about advising you, for I am only a boy, but I should think you would give up such a dangerous habit."

"Say no more, Carl! You are a true friend. I will try to follow your advice. Give me your hand."

Carl did so, and felt a warm glow of pleasure at the thought that perhaps he had redeemed his companion from a fascinating vice.

"I really wish I had a sensible boy like you to be my constant companion. I should feel safer."

"Do you really have such a passion for gambling, then?"

"Yes; if at the hotel to-night I should see a party playing poker, I could not resist joining them. Odd, isn't it?"

"I am glad I have no such temptation."

"Yes, you are lucky. By the way, how much money have you about you?"

"Five dollars."

"Then you can do me a favor. I have a ten-dollar bill, which I need to get me home. Now, I would like to have you keep a part of it for me till I go away in the morning. Give me your five, and I will hand you ten. Out of that you can pay my hotel bill and hand me the balance due me in the morning."

"If you really wish me to do so."

"Enough said. Here is the ten."

Carl took the bill, and gave Mr. Hubbard his five-dollar note.

"You are placing considerable confidence in me," he said.

"I am, it is true, but I have no fear of being deceived. You are a boy who naturally inspires confidence."

Carl thought Mr. Chauncy Hubbard a very agreeable and sensible fellow, and he felt flattered to think that the young man had chosen him as a guardian, so to speak.

"By the way, Carl, you haven't told me," said Hubbard, as they pursued their journey, "how a boy like yourself is forced to work his own way."

"I can tell you the reason very briefly - I have a stepmother."

"I understand. Is your father living?"

"Yes."

"But he thinks more of the stepmother than of you?"

"I am afraid he does."

"You have my sympathy, Carl. I will do all I can to help you. If you can only get a place in our establishment, you will be all right. Step by step you will rise, till you come to stand where I do."

"That would satisfy me. Has Mr. Brandes got another daughter?"

"No, there is only one."

"Then I shall have to be content with the forty dollars a week. If I ever get it, I will save half."

"I wish I could."

"You can if you try. Why, you might have two thousand dollars saved up now, if you had only begun to save in time."

"I have lost more than that at the gaming table. You will think me very foolish."

"Yes, I do," said Carl, frankly.

"You are right. But here we are almost at the village."

"Is there a good hotel?"

"Yes - the Fillmore. We will take adjoining rooms if you say so."

"Very well."

"And in the morning you will pay the bill?"

"Certainly."

The two travelers had a good supper, and retired early, both being fatigued with the journey. It was not till eight o'clock the next morning that Carl opened his eyes. He dressed hastily, and went down to breakfast. He was rather surprised not to see his companion of the day before.

"Has Mr. Hubbard come down yet?" he asked at the desk.

"Yes; he took an early breakfast, and went off by the first train."

"That is strange. I was to pay his bill."

"He paid it himself."

Carl did not know what to make of this. Had Hubbard forgotten that he had five dollars belonging to him? Fortunately, Carl had his city address, and could refund the money in New York.

"Very well! I will pay my own bill. How much is it?"

"A dollar and a quarter."

Carl took the ten-dollar bill from his wallet and tendered it to the clerk.

Instead of changing it at once, the clerk held it up to the light and examined it critically.

"I can't take that bill," he said, abruptly.

"Why not?"

"Because it is counterfeit."

Carl turned pale, and the room seemed to whirl round. It was all the money he had.

CHAPTER X.

THE COUNTERFEIT BILL.

"Are you sure it is counterfeit?" asked Carl, very much disturbed.

"I am certain of it. I haven't been handling bank bills for ten years without being able to tell good money from bad. I'll trouble you for another bill."

"That's all the money I have," faltered Carl.

"Look here, young man," said the clerk, sternly, "you are trying a bold game, but it won't succeed."

"I am trying no game at all," said Carl, plucking up spirit. "I thought the bill was good."

"Where did you get it?"

"From the man who came with me last evening - Mr. Hubbard."

"The money he gave me was good."

"What did he give you?"

"A five-dollar bill."

"It was my five-dollar bill," said Carl, bitterly.

"Your story doesn't seem very probable," said the clerk, suspiciously. "How did he happen to get your money, and you his?"

"He told me that he would get to gambling, and wished me to take money enough to pay his bill here. He handed me the ten-dollar bill which you say is bad, and I gave him five in return. I think now he only wanted to get good money for bad."

"Your story may be true, or it may not," said the clerk, whose manner indicated incredulity. "That is nothing to me. All you have to do is to pay your hotel bill, and you can settle with Mr. Hubbard when you see him."

"But I have no other money," said Carl, desperately.

"Then I shall feel justified in ordering your arrest on a charge of passing, or trying to pass, counterfeit money."

"Don't do that, sir! I will see that you are paid out of the first money I earn."

"You must think I am soft," said the clerk, contemptuously. "I have seen persons of your tripe before. I dare say, if you were searched, more counterfeit money would be found in your pockets."

"Search me, then!" cried Carl, indignantly. "I am perfectly willing that you should."

"Haven't you any relations who will pay your bill?"

"I have no one to call upon," answered Carl, soberly. "Couldn't you let me work it out? I am ready to do any kind of work."

"Our list of workers is full," said the clerk, coldly.

Poor Carl! he felt that he was decidedly in a tight place. He had never before found himself unable to meet his bills. nor would he have been so placed now but for Hubbard's rascality. A dollar and a quarter seems a small sum, but if you are absolutely penniless it might as well be a thousand. Suppose he should be arrested and the story get into the papers? How his stepmother would exult in the record of his disgrace! He could anticipate what she would say. Peter, too, would rejoice, and between them both his father would be persuaded that he was thoroughly unprincipled.

"What have you got in your valise?" asked the clerk.

"Only some underclothing. If there were anything of any value I would cheerfully leave it as security. Wait a minute, though," he said, with a sudden thought. "Here is a gold pencil! It is worth five dollars; at any rate, it cost more than that. I can place that in your hands."

"Let me see it."

Carl handed the clerk a neat gold pencil, on which his name was inscribed. It was evidently of good quality, and found favor with the clerk.

"I'll give you a dollar and a quarter for the pencil," he said, "and call it square."

"I wouldn't like to sell it," said Carl.

"You won't get any more for it."

"I wasn't thinking of that; but it was given me by my mother, who is now dead. I would not like to part with anything that she gave me."

"You would prefer to get off scot-free, I suppose?" retorted the clerk, with a sneer.

"No; I am willing to leave it in your hands, but I should like the privilege of redeeming it when I have the money."

"Very well," said the clerk, who reflected that in all probability Carl would never come back for it. "I'll take it on those conditions."

Carl passed over the pencil with a sigh. He didn't like to part with it, even for a short time, but there seemed no help for it.

"All right. I will mark you paid."

Carl left the hotel, satchel in hand, and as he passed out into the street, reflected with a sinking heart that he was now quite penniless. Where was he to get his dinner, and how was he to provide himself with a lodging that night? At present he was not hungry, having eaten a hearty breakfast at the hotel, but by one o'clock he would feel the need of food. He began to ask himself if, after all, he had not been unwise in leaving home, no matter how badly he had been treated by his stepmother. There, at least, he was certain of living comfortably. Now he was in danger of starvation, and on two occasions already he had incurred suspicion, once of being concerned in a murder, and just now of passing counterfeit money. Ought he to have submitted, and so avoided all these perils?

"No!" he finally decided; "I won't give up the ship yet. I am about as badly off as I can be; I am without a cent, and don't know where my next meal is to come from. But my luck may turn - it must turn - it has turned!" he exclaimed with energy, as his wandering glance suddenly fell upon a silver quarter of a dollar, nearly covered up with the dust of the street. "That shall prove a good omen!"

He stooped over and picked up the coin, which he put in his vest pocket.

It was wonderful how the possession of this small sum of money restored his courage and raised his spirits. He was sure of a dinner now, at all events. It looked as if Providence was smiling on him.

Two miles farther on Carl overtook a boy of about his own age trudging along the road with a rake over his shoulder. He wore overalls, and was evidently a farmer's boy.

"Good-day!" said Carl, pleasantly, noticing that the boy regarded him with interest.

"Good-day!" returned the country lad, rather bashfully.

"Can you tell me if there is any place near where I can buy some dinner?"

"There ain't no tavern, if that's what you mean. I'm goin' home to dinner myself."

"Where do you live?"

"Over yonder."

He pointed to a farmhouse about a dozen rods away.

"Do you think your mother would give me some dinner?"

"I guess she would. Mam's real accommodatin'."

"Will you ask her?"

"Yes; just come along of me."

He turned into the yard, and followed a narrow path to the back door.

"I'll stay here while you ask," said Carl.

The boy entered the house, and came out after a brief absence.

"Mam says you're to come in," he said.

Carl, glad at heart, and feeling quite prepared to eat fifty cents' worth of dinner, followed the boy inside.

A pleasant-looking, matronly woman, plainly but neatly attired, came forward to greet him.

"Nat says you would like to get some dinner," she said.

"Yes," answered Carl. "I hope you'll excuse my applying to you, but your son tells me there is no hotel near by."

"The nearest one is three miles away from here."

"I don't think I can hold out so long," said Carl, smiling.

"Sit right down with Nat," said the farmer's wife, hospitably. "Mr. Sweetser won't be home for half an hour. We've got enough, such as it is."

Evidently Mrs. Sweetser was a good cook. The dinner consisted of boiled mutton, with several kinds of vegetables. A cup of tea and two kinds of pie followed.

It was hard to tell which of the two boys did fuller justice to the meal. Nat had the usual appetite of a healthy farm boy, and Carl, in spite of his recent anxieties, and narrow escape from serious peril, did not allow himself to fall behind.

"Your mother's a fine cook!" said Carl, between two mouthfuls.

"Ain't she, though?" answered Nat, his mouth full of pie.

When Carl rose from the table he feared that he had eaten more than his little stock of money would pay for.

"How much will it be, Mrs. Sweetser?" he asked.

"Oh, you're quite welcome to all you've had,"

said the good woman, cheerily. "It's plain farmer's fare."

"I never tasted a better dinner," said Carl.

Mrs. Sweetser seemed pleased with the compliment to her cooking.

"Come again when you are passing this way," she said. "You will always be welcome to a dinner."

Carl thanked her heartily, and pressed on his way. Two hours later, at a lonely point of the road, an ill-looking tramp, who had been reclining by the wayside, jumped up, and addressed him in a menacing tone:

"Young feller, shell over all the money you have got, or I'll hurt you! I'm hard up, and I won't stand no nonsense."

Carl started and looked into the face of the tramp. It seemed to him that he had never seen a man more ill-favored, or villainous-looking.

CHAPTER XI.

THE ARCHERY PRIZE.

Situated as he was, it seemed, on second thought, rather a joke to Carl to be attacked by a robber. He had but twenty-five cents in good money about him, and that he had just picked up by the merest chance.

"Do I look like a banker?" he asked, humorously. "Why do you want to rob a boy?"

"The way you're togged out, you must have something," growled the tramp, "and I haven't got a penny."

"Your business doesn't seem to pay, then?"

"Don't you make fun of me, or I'll wring your neck! Just hand over your money and be quick about it! I haven't time to stand fooling here all day."

A bright idea came to Carl. He couldn't spare the silver coin, which constituted all his available wealth, but he still had the counterfeit note.

"You won't take all my money, will you?" he said, earnestly.

"How much have you got?" asked the tramp, pricking

up his ears.

Carl, with apparent reluctance, drew out the ten-dollar bill.

The tramp's face lighted up.

"Is your name Vanderbilt?" he asked. "I didn't expect to make such a haul."

"Can't you give me back a dollar out of it? I don't want to lose all I have."

"I haven't got a cent. You'll have to wait till we meet again. So long, boy! You've helped me out of a scrape."

"Or into one," thought Carl.

The tramp straightened up, buttoned his dilapidated coat, and walked off with the consciousness of being a capitalist.

Carl watched him with a smile.

"I hope I won't meet him after he has discovered that the bill is a counterfeit," he said to himself.

He congratulated himself upon being still the possessor of twenty-five cents in silver. It was not much, but it seemed a great deal better than being penniless. A week before he would have thought it impossible that such a paltry sum would have made him feel comfortable, but he had passed through a great deal since then.

Horatio Alger, Jr.

About the middle of the afternoon he came to a field, in which something appeared to be going on. Some forty or fifty young persons, boys and girls, were walking about the grass, and seemed to be preparing for some interesting event.

Carl stopped to rest and look on.

"What's going on here?" he asked of a boy who was sitting on the fence.

"It's a meeting of the athletic association," said the boy.

"What are they doing?"

"They try for prizes in jumping, vaulting, archery and so on."

This interested Carl, who excelled in all manly exercises.

"I suppose I may stay and look on?" he said, inquiringly.

"Why, of course. Jump over the fence and I'll go round with you."

It seemed pleasant to Carl to associate once more with boys of his own age. Thrown unexpectedly upon his own resources, he had almost forgotten that he was a boy. Face to face with a cold and unsympathizing world, he seemed to himself twenty-five at least.

"Those who wish to compete for the archery prize will come forward," announced Robert Gardiner, a young man of nineteen, who, as Carl learned, was the president of the association. "You all understand the conditions. The entry fee to competitors is ten cents. The prize to the most successful archer is one dollar."

Several boys came forward and paid the entrance fee.

"Would you like to compete?" asked Edward Downie, the boy whose acquaintance Carl had made.

"I am an outsider," said Carl. "I don't belong to the association."

"I'll speak to the president, if you like."

"I don't want to intrude."

"It won't be considered an intrusion. You pay the entrance fee and take your chances."

Edward went to the president and spoke to him in a low voice. The result was that he advanced to Carl, and said, courteously:

"If you would like to enter into our games, you are quite at liberty to do so."

"Thank you," responded Carl. "I have had a little practice in archery, and will enter my name for that prize."

He paid over his quarter and received back fifteen cents in change. It seemed rather an imprudent outlay, considering his small capital; but he had good hopes of carrying off the prize, and that would be a great lift for him. Seven boys entered besides Carl. The first was Victor Russell, a lad of fourteen, whose arrow went three feet above the mark.

"The prize is mine if none of you do better than that," laughed Victor, good-naturedly.

"I hope not, for the credit of the club," said the president. "Mr. Crawford, will you shoot next?"

"I would prefer to be the last," said Carl, modestly.

"John Livermore, your turn now."

John came a little nearer than his predecessor, but did not distinguish himself.

"If that is a specimen of the skill of the clubmen," thought Carl, "my chance is a good one."

Next came Frank Stockton, whose arrow stuck only three inches from the center of the target.

"Good for Fred!" cried Edward Downie. "Just wait till you see me shoot!"

"Are you a dangerous rival?" asked Carl, smiling.

"I can hit a barn door if I am only near enough," replied Edward.

"Edward Downie!" called the president.

Edward took his bow and advanced to the proper place, bent it, and the arrow sped on its way.

There was a murmur of surprise when his arrow struck only an inch to the right of the centre. No one was more amazed than Edward himself, for he was accounted far from skillful. It was indeed a lucky accident.

"What do you say to that?" asked Edward, triumphantly.

"I think the prize is yours. I had no idea you could shoot like that," said Carl.

"Nor I," rejoined Edward, laughing.

"Carl Crawford!" called the president.

Carl took his position, and bent his bow with the greatest care. He exercised unusual deliberation, for success meant more to him than to any of the others. A dollar to him in his present circumstances would be a small fortune, while the loss of even ten cents would be sensibly felt. His heart throbbed with excitement as he let the arrow speed on its mission.

His unusual deliberation, and the fact that he was a stranger, excited strong interest, and all eyes followed the arrow with eager attentiveness.

There was a sudden shout of irrepressible excitement.

Carl's arrow had struck the bull's-eye and the prize was his.

"Christopher!" exclaimed Edward Downie, "you've beaten me, after all!"

"I'm almost sorry," said Carl, apologetically, but the light in his eyes hardly bore out the statement.

"Never mind. Everybody would have called it a fluke if I had won," said Edward. "I expect to get the prize for the long jump. I am good at that."

"So am I, but I won't compete; I will leave it to you."

"No, no. I want to win fair."

Carl accordingly entered his name. He made the second best jump, but Edward's exceeded his by a couple of inches, and the prize was adjudged to him.

"I have my revenge," he said, smiling. "I am glad I won, for it wouldn't have been to the credit of the club to have an outsider carry off two prizes."

"I am perfectly satisfied," said Carl; "I ought to be, for I did not expect to carry off any."

Carl decided not to compete for any other prize. He had invested twenty cents and got back a dollar, which left him a profit of eighty cents. This, with his original quarter, made him the possessor of a dollar and five cents.

"My luck seems to have turned," he said to himself, and the thought gave him fresh courage.

It was five o'clock when the games were over, and Carl prepared to start again on his journey.

"Where are you going to take supper?" asked Downie.

"I - don't - know."

"Come home with me. If you are in no hurry, you may

as well stay overnight, and go on in the morning."

"Are you sure it won't inconvenience you?"

"Not at all."

"Then I'll accept with thanks."

CHAPTER XII.

AN ODD ACQUAINTANCE.

After breakfast the next morning Carl started again on his way. His new friend, Edward Downie, accompanied him for a mile, having an errand at that distance.

"I wish you good luck, Carl," he said, earnestly. "When you come this way again, be sure to stop in and see me."

"I will certainly do so, but I hope I may find employment."

"At any rate," thought Carl, as he resumed his journey alone, "I am better off than I was yesterday morning. Then I had but twenty-five cents; now I have a dollar."

This was satisfactory as far as it went, but Carl was sensible that he was making no progress in his plan of earning a living. He was simply living from hand to mouth, and but for good luck he would have had to go hungry, and perhaps have been obliged to sleep out doors. What he wanted was employment.

It was about ten o'clock when, looking along the road, his curiosity was excited by a man of very unusual figure a few rods in advance of him. He looked no taller than a boy of ten; but his frame was large, his shoulders broad, and his arms were of unusual length. He might properly be called a dwarf.

"I am glad I am not so small as that," thought Carl. "I am richer than he in having a good figure. I should not like to excite attention wherever I go by being unusually large or unusually small."

Some boys would have felt inclined to laugh at the queer figure, but Carl had too much good feeling. His curiosity certainly was aroused, and he thought he would like to get acquainted with the little man, whose garments of fine texture showed that, though short in stature, he was probably long in purse. He didn't quite know how to pave the way for an acquaintance, but circumstances favored him.

The little man drew out a handkerchief from the side pocket of his overcoat. With it fluttered out a bank bill, which fell to the ground apparently unobserved by the owner.

Carl hurried on, and, picking up the bill, said to the small stranger as he touched his arm: "Here is some money you just dropped, sir."

The little man turned round and smiled pleasantly.

"Thank you. Are you sure it is mine?"

"Yes, sir; it came out with your handkerchief."

"Let me see. So it is mine. I was very careless to put it loose in my pocket."

"You were rather careless, sir."

"Of what denomination is it?'

"It is a two-dollar note."

"If you had been a poor boy," said the little man, eying Carl keenly, "you might have been tempted to keep it. I might not have known."

Carl smiled.

"What makes you think I am not a poor boy?" he said.

"You are well dressed."

"That is true; but all the money I have is a dollar and five cents."

"You know where to get more? You have a good home?"

"I had a home, but now I am thrown on my own exertions," said Carl, soberly.

"Dear me! That is bad! If I were better acquainted, I might ask more particularly how this happens. Are you an orphan?"

"No, sir; my father is living."

"And your mother is dead?"

"Yes, sir."

"Is your father a poor man?"

"No, sir; he is moderately rich."

"Yet you have to fight your own way?"

"Yes, sir. I have a stepmother."

"I see. Are you sure you are not unreasonably prejudiced against your stepmother? All stepmothers are not bad or unkind."

"I know that, sir."

"Yours is, I presume?"

"You can judge for yourself."

Carl recited some incidents in his experience with his stepmother. The stranger listened with evident interest.

"I am not in general in favor of boys leaving home except on extreme provocation," he said, after a pause; "but in your case, as your father seems to take part against you, I think you may be justified, especially as, at your age, you have a fair chance of making your own living."

"I am glad you think that, sir. I have begun to wonder whether I have not acted rashly."

"In undertaking to support yourself?"

"Yes, sir."

"How old are you?"

"Sixteen."

"At fourteen I was obliged to undertake what you have now before you."

"To support yourself?"

"Yes; I was left an orphan at fourteen, with no money left me by my poor father, and no relatives who could help me."

"How did you make out, sir?" asked Carl, feeling very much interested.

"I sold papers for a while - in Newark, New Jersey - then I got a place at three dollars a week, out of which I had to pay for board, lodging and clothes. Well, I won't go through my history. I will only say that whatever I did I did as well as I could. I am now a man of about middle age, and I am moderately wealthy."

"I am very much encouraged by what you tell me, sir."

"Perhaps you don't understand what a hard struggle I had. More than once I have had to go to bed hungry. Sometimes I have had to sleep out, but one mustn't be afraid to rough it a little when he is young. I shouldn't like to sleep out now, or go to bed without my supper," and the little man laughed softly.

"Yes, sir; I expect to rough it, but if I could only get a situation, at no matter what income, I should feel encouraged."

"You have earned no money yet?"

"Yes, sir; I earned a dollar yesterday."

"At what kind of work?"

"Archery."

The little man looked surprised.

"Is that a business?" he asked, curiously.

"I'll explain how it was," and Carl told about the contest.

"So you hit the mark?" said the little man, significantly.

Somehow, there was something in the little man's tone that put new courage into Carl, and incited him to fresh effort.

"I wonder, sir," he said, after a pause, "that you should be walking, when you can well afford to ride."

The little man smiled.

"It is by advice of my physician," he said. "He tells me I am getting too stout, and ought to take more or less exercise in the open air. So I am trying to follow his advice "

"Are you in business near here, sir?"

"At a large town six miles distant. I may not walk all the way there, but I have a place to call at near by, and thought I would avail myself of the good chance offered to take a little exercise. I feel repaid. I have made a pleasant acquaintance."

"Thank you, sir."

"There is my card," and the little man took out a business card, reading thus:

HENRY JENNINGS,
FURNITURE WAREHOUSE,
MILFORD.

"I manufacture my furniture in the country," he continued, "but I ship it by special arrangements to a house in New York in which I am also interested."

"Yes, sir, I see. Do you employ many persons in your establishment?"

"About thirty."

"Do you think you could make room for me?"

"Do you think you would like the business?"

"I am prepared to like any business in which I can make a living."

"That is right. That is the way to look at it. Let me think."

For two minutes Mr. Jennings seemed to be plunged in thought. Then he turned and smiled encouragingly.

"You can come home with me," he said, "and I will consider the matter."

"Thank you, sir," said Carl, gladly.

"I have got to make a call at the next house, not on business, though. There is an old schoolmate lying there sick. I am afraid he is rather poor, too. You can walk on slowly, and I will overtake you in a few minutes."

"Thank you, sir."

"After walking half a mile, if I have not overtaken you, you may sit down under a tree and wait for me."

"All right, sir."

"Before I leave you I will tell you a secret."

"What is it, sir?"

"The two dollars you picked up, I dropped on purpose."

"On purpose?" asked Carl, in amazement.

"Yes; I wanted to try you, to see if you were honest."

"Then you had noticed me?"

"Yes. I liked your appearance, but I wanted to test you."

CHAPTER XIII.

AN UNEQUAL CONTEST.

Carl walked on slowly. He felt encouraged by the prospect of work, for he was sure that Mr. Jennings would make a place for him, if possible.

"He is evidently a kind-hearted man," Carl reflected. "Besides, he has been poor himself, and he can sympathize with me. The wages may be small, but I won't mind that, if I only support myself economically, and get on." To most boys brought up in comfort, not to say luxury, the prospect of working hard for small pay would not have seemed inviting. But Carl was essentially manly, and had sensible ideas about labor. It was no sacrifice or humiliation to him to become a working boy, for he had never considered himself superior to working boys, as many boys in his position would have done.

He walked on in a leisurely manner, and at the end of ten minutes thought he had better sit down and wait for Mr. Jennings. But he was destined to receive a shock. There, under the tree which seemed to offer the most inviting shelter, reclined a figure only too well-known.

It was the tramp who the day before had compelled him to surrender the ten-dollar bill.

The ill-looking fellow glanced up, and when his gaze rested upon Carl, his face beamed with savage joy.

"So it's you, is it?" he said, rising from his seat.

"Yes," answered Carl, doubtfully.

"Do you remember me?"

"Yes."

"I have cause to remember you, my chicken. That was a mean trick you played upon me," and he nodded his head significantly.

"I should think it was you that played the trick on me."

"How do you make that out?" growled the tramp.

"You took my money."

"So I did, and much good it did me."

Carl was silent.

"You know why, don't you?"

Carl might have denied that he knew the character of the bill which was stolen from him, but I am glad to say that it would have come from him with a very ill grace, for he was accustomed to tell the truth under all circumstances.

"You knew that the bill was counterfeit, didn't you?" demanded the tramp, fiercely.

"I was told so at the hotel where I offered it in payment for my bill."

"Yet you passed it on me!"

"I didn't pass it on you. You took it from me," retorted Carl, with spirit.

"That makes no difference."

"I think it does. I wouldn't have offered it to anyone in payment of an honest bill."

"Humph! you thought because I was poor and unfortunate you could pass it off on me!"

This seemed so grotesque that Carl found it difficult not to laugh.

"Do you know it nearly got me into trouble?" went on the tramp.

"How was that?"

"I stopped at a baker's shop to get a lunch. When I got through I offered the bill. The old Dutchman put on his spectacles, and he looked first at the bill, then at me. Then he threatened to have me arrested for passing bad money. I told him I'd go out in the back yard and settle it with him. I tell you, boy, I'd have knocked him out in one round, and he knew it, so he bade me be gone and never darken his door again. Where did you get it?"

"It was passed on me by a man I was traveling with."

"How much other money have you got?" asked the tramp.

"Very little."

"Give it to me, whatever it is."

This was a little too much for Carl's patience.

"I have no money to spare," he said, shortly.

"Say that over again!" said the tramp, menacingly.

"If you don't understand me, I will. I have no money to spare."

"You'll spare it to me, I reckon."

"Look here," said Carl, slowly backing. "You've robbed me of ten dollars. You'll have to be satisfied with that."

"It was no good. It might have sent me to prison. If I was nicely dressed I might pass it, but when a chap like me offers a ten-dollar bill it's sure to he looked at sharply. I haven't a cent, and I'll trouble you to hand over all you've got."

"Why don't you work for a living? You are a strong, able-bodied man."

"You'll find I am if you give me any more of your palaver."

Carl saw that the time of negotiation was past, and that active hostilities were about to commence.

Horatio Alger, Jr.

Accordingly he turned and ran, not forward, but in the reverse direction, hoping in this way to meet with Mr. Jennings.

"Ah, that's your game, is it?" growled the tramp. "You needn't expect to escape, for I'll overhaul you in two minutes."

So Carl ran, and his rough acquaintance ran after him.

It could hardly be expected that a boy of sixteen, though stout and strong, could get away from a tall, powerful man like the tramp.

Looking back over his shoulder, Carl saw that the tramp was but three feet behind, and almost able to lay his hand upon his shoulder.

He dodged dexterously, and in trying to do the same the tramp nearly fell to the ground. Naturally, this did not sweeten his temper.

"I'll half murder you when I get hold of you," he growled, in a tone that bodied ill for Carl.

The latter began to pant, and felt that he could not hold out much longer. Should he surrender at discretion?

"If some one would only come along," was his inward aspiration. "This man will take my money and beat me, too."

As if in reply to his fervent prayer the small figure of Mr. Jennings appeared suddenly, rounding a curve in the road.

"Save me, save me, Mr. Jennings!" cried Carl, running up to the little man for protection.

"What is the matter? Who is this fellow?" asked Mr. Jennings, in a deep voice for so small a man.

"That tramp wants to rob me."

"Don't trouble yourself! He won't do it," said Jennings, calmly.

CHAPTER XIV.

CARL ARRIVES IN MILFORD.

The tramp stopped short, and eyed Carl's small defender, first with curious surprise, and then with derision.

"Out of my way, you midget!" he cried, "or 'll hurt you."

"Try it!" said the little man, showing no sign of fear.

"Why, you're no bigger than a kid. I can upset you with one finger."

He advanced contemptuously, and laid his hand on the shoulder of the dwarf. In an instant Jennings had swung his flail-like arms, and before the tramp understood what was happening he was lying flat on his back, as much to Carl's amazement as his own.

He leaped to his feet with an execration, and advanced again to the attack. To be upset by such a pigmy was the height of mortification.

"I'm going to crush you, you mannikin!" he threatened.

Jennings put himself on guard. Like many small men,

he was very powerful, as his broad shoulders and sinewy arms would have made evident to a teacher of gymnastics. He clearly understood that this opponent was in deadly earnest, and he put out all the strength which he possessed. The result was that his large-framed antagonist went down once more, striking his head with a force that nearly stunned him.

It so happened that at this juncture reinforcements arrived. A sheriff and his deputy drove up in an open buggy, and, on witnessing the encounter, halted their carriage and sprang to the ground.

"What is the matter, Mr. Jennings?" asked the sheriff, respectfully, for the little man was a person of importance in that vicinity.

"That gentleman is trying to extort a forced loan, Mr. Clunningham."

"Ha! a footpad?"

"Yes."

The sheriff sprang to the side of the tramp, who was trying to rise, and in a trice his wrists were confined by handcuffs.

"I think I know you, Mike Frost," he said. "You are up to your old tricks. When did you come out of Sing Sing?"

"Three weeks since," answered the tramp, sullenly.

"They want you back there. Come along with me!"

He was assisted into the buggy, and spent that night in the lockup.

"Did he take anything from you, Carl?" asked Mr. Jennings.

"No, sir; but I was in considerable danger. How strong you are!" he added, admiringly.

"Strength isn't always according to size!" said the little man, quietly. "Nature gave me a powerful, though small, frame, and I have increased my strength by gymnastic exercise."

Mr. Jennings did not show the least excitement after his desperate contest. He had attended to it as a matter of business, and when over he suffered it to pass out of his mind. He took out his watch and noted the time.

"It is later than I thought," he said. "I think I shall have to give up my plan of walking the rest of the way."

"Then I shall be left alone," thought Carl regretfully.

Just then a man overtook them in a carriage.

He greeted Mr. Jennings respectfully.

"Are you out for a long walk?" he said.

"Yes, but I find time is passing too rapidly with me. Are you going to Milford?"

"Yes, sir."

"Can you take two passengers?"

"You and the boy?"

"Yes; of course I will see that you don't lose by it."

"I ought not to charge you anything, Mr. Jennings. Several times you have done me favors."

"And I hope to again, but this is business. If a dollar will pay you, the boy and I will ride with you."

"It will be so much gain, as I don't go out of my way."

"You can take the back seat, Carl," said Mr. Jennings. "I will sit with Mr. Leach."

They were soon seated and on their way.

"Relative of yours, Mr. Jennings?" asked Leach, with a backward glance at Carl.

Like most country folks, he was curious about people. Those who live in cities meet too many of their kind to feel an interest in strangers.

"No; a young friend," answered Jennings, briefly.

"Goin' to visit you?"

"Yes, I think he will stay with me for a time."

Then the conversation touched upon Milford matters in which at present Carl was not interested.

After his fatiguing walk our hero enjoyed the sensation of riding. The road was a pleasant one, the day was bright with sunshine and the air vocal with the songs of birds. For a time houses were met at rare intervals, but after a while it became evident that they were approaching a town of considerable size.

"Is this Milford, Mr. Jennings?" asked Carl.

"Yes," answered the little man, turning with a pleasant smile.

"How large is it?"

"I think there are twelve thousand inhabitants. It is what Western people call a `right smart place.' It has been my home for twenty years, and I am much attached to it."

"And it to you, Mr. Jennings," put in the driver.

"That is pleasant to hear," said Jennings, with a smile.

"It is true. There are few people here whom you have not befriended."

"That is what we are here for, is it not?"

"I wish all were of your opinion. Why, Mr. Jennings, when we get a city charter I think I know who will be the first mayor."

"Not I, Mr. Leach. My own business is all I can well attend to. Thank you for your compliment, though. Carl, do you see yonder building?"

He pointed to a three-story structure, a frame building, occupying a prominent position.

"Yes, sir."

"That is my manufactory. What do you think of it?"

"I shouldn't think a town of this size would require so large an establishment," answered Carl.

Mr. Jennings laughed.

"You are right," he said. "If I depended on Milford trade, a very small building would be sufficient. My trade is outside. I supply many dealers in New York City and at the West. My retail trade is small. If any of my neighbors want furniture they naturally come to me, and I favor them as to price out of friendly feeling, but I am a manufacturer and wholesale dealer."

"I see, sir."

"Shall I take you to your house, Mr. Jennings?" asked Leach.

"Yes, if you please."

Leach drove on till he reached a two-story building of Quaker-like simplicity but with a large, pleasant yard in front, with here and there a bed of flowers. Here he stopped his horse.

"We have reached our destination, Carl," said Mr. Jennings. "You are active. Jump out and I will follow."

Carl needed no second invitation. He sprang from the carriage and went forward to help Mr. Jennings out.

"No, thank you, Carl," said the little man. "I am more

active than you think. Here we are!"

He descended nimbly to the ground, and, drawing a one-dollar bill from his pocket, handed it to the driver.

"I don't like to take it, Mr. Jennings," said Mr. Leach.

"Why not? The laborer is worthy of his hire. Now, Carl, let us go into the house."

CHAPTER XV.

Mr. JENNINGS AT HOME.

Mr. Jennings did not need to open the door. He had scarcely set foot on the front step when it was opened from inside, and Carl found a fresh surprise in store for him. A woman, apparently six feet in height, stood on the threshold. Her figure was spare and ungainly, and her face singularly homely, but the absence of beauty was partially made up by a kindly expression. She looked with some surprise at Carl.

"This is a young friend of mine, Hannah," said her master. "Welcome him for my sake."

"I am glad to see you," said Hannah, in a voice that was another amazement. It was deeper than that of most men.

As she spoke, she held out a large masculine hand, which Carl took, as seemed to be expected.

"Thank you," said Carl.

"What am I to call you?" asked Hannah.

"Carl Crawford."

"That's a strange name."

"It is not common, I believe."

"You two will get acquainted by and by," said Mr. Jennings. "The most interesting question at present is, when will dinner be ready?"

"In ten minutes," answered Hannah, promptly.

"Carl and I are both famished. We have had considerable exercise," here he nodded at Carl with a comical look, and Carl understood that he referred in part to his contest with the tramp.

Hannah disappeared into the kitchen, and Mr. Jennings said: "Come upstairs, Carl. I will show you your room."

Up an old-fashioned stairway Carl followed his host, and the latter opened the door of a side room on the first landing. It was not large, but was neat and comfortable. There was a cottage bedstead, a washstand, a small bureau and a couple of chairs.

"I hope you will come to feel at home here," said Mr. Jennings, kindly.

"Thank you, sir. I am sure I shall," Carl responded, gratefully.

"There are some nails to hang your clothing on," went on Mr. Jennings, and then he stopped short, for it was clear that Carl's small gripsack could not contain an extra suit, and he felt delicate at calling up in the boy's mind the thought of his poverty.

"Thank you, sir," said Carl. "I left my trunk at the house of a friend, and if you should succeed in finding me a place, I will send for it."

"That is well!" returned Mr. Jennings, looking relieved. "Now I will leave you for a few moments. You will find water and towels, in case you wish to wash before dinner."

Carl was glad of the opportunity. He was particular about his personal appearance, and he felt hot and dusty. He bathed his face and hands, carefully dusted his suit, brushed his hair, and was ready to descend when he heard the tinkling of a small bell at the foot of the front stairs.

He readily found his way into the neat dining-room at the rear of the parlor. Mr. Jennings sat at the head of the table, a little giant, diminutive in stature, but with broad shoulders, a large head, and a powerful frame. Opposite him sat Hannah, tall, stiff and upright as a grenadier. She formed a strange contrast to her employer.

"I wonder what made him hire such a tall woman?" thought Carl. "Being so small himself, her size makes him look smaller."

There was a chair at one side, placed for Carl.

"Sit down there, Carl," said Mr. Jennings. "I won't keep you waiting any longer than I can help. What have you given us to-day, Hannah?"

"Roast beef," answered Hannah in her deep tones.

"There is nothing better."

The host cut off a liberal slice for Carl, and passed the plate to Hannah, who supplied potatoes, peas and squash. Carl's mouth fairly watered as he watched the hospitable preparations for his refreshment.

"I never trouble myself about what we are to have on the table," said Mr. Jennings. "Hannah always sees to that. She's knows just what I want. She is a capital cook, too, Hannah is."

Hannah looked pleased at this compliment.

"You are easily pleased, master," she said.

"I should be hard to suit if I were not pleased with your cooking. You don't know so well Carl's taste, but if there is anything he likes particularly he can tell you."

"You are very kind, sir," said Carl.

"There are not many men who would treat a poor boy so considerately," he thought. "He makes me an honored guest."

When dinner was over, Mr. Jennings invited Carl to accompany him on a walk. They passed along the principal street, nearly every person they met giving the little man a cordial greeting.

"He seems to be very popular," thought Carl.

At length they reached the manufactory. Mr. Jennings went into the office, followed by Carl.

A slender, dark-complexioned man, about thirty-five years of age, sat on a stool at a high desk. He was evidently the bookkeeper.

"Any letters, Mr. Gibbon?" asked Mr. Jennings.

"Yes, sir; here are four."

"Where are they from?"

"From New York, Chicago, Pittsburg and New Haven."

"What do they relate to?"

"Orders. I have handed them to Mr. Potter."

Potter, as Carl afterwards learned, was superintendent of the manufactory, and had full charge of practical details.

"Is there anything requiring my personal attention?"

"No, sir; I don't think so."

"By the way, Mr. Gibbon, let me introduce you to a young friend of mine - Carl Crawford."

The bookkeeper rapidly scanned Carl's face and figure. It seemed to Carl that the scrutiny was not a friendly one.

"I am glad to see you," said Mr. Gibbon, coldly.

"Thank you, sir."

"By the way, Mr. Jennings," said the bookkeeper, "I have a favor to ask of you."

"Go on, Mr. Gibbon," rejoined his employer, in a cordial tone.

"Two months since you gave my nephew, Leonard Craig, a place in the factory."

"Yes; I remember."

"I don't think the work agrees with him."

"He seemed a strong, healthy boy."

"He has never been used to confinement, and it affects him unpleasantly."

"Does he wish to resign his place?"

"I have been wondering whether you would not be willing to transfer him to the office. I could send him on errands, to the post office, and make him useful in various ways."

"I had not supposed an office boy was needed. Still, if you desire it, I will try your nephew in the place."

"Thank you, sir."

"I am bound to tell you, however, that his present place is a better one. He is learning a good trade, which, if he masters it, will always give him a livelihood. I learned a trade, and owe all I have to that."

"True, Mr. Jennings, but there are other ways of

earning a living."

"Certainly."

"And I thought of giving Leonard evening instruction in bookkeeping."

"That alters the case. Good bookkeepers are always in demand. I have no objection to your trying the experiment."

"Thank you, sir."

"Have you mentioned the matter to your nephew?"

"I just suggested that I would ask you, but could not say what answer you would give."

"It would have been better not to mention the matter at all till you could tell him definitely that he could change his place."

"I don't know but you are right, sir. However, it is all right now."

"Now, Carl," said Mr. Jennings, "I will take you into the workroom."

Horatio Alger, Jr.

CHAPTER XVI.

CARL GETS A PLACE.

"I suppose that is the bookkeeper," said Carl.

"Yes. He has been with me three years. He understands his business well. You heard what he said about his nephew?"

"Yes, sir."

"It is his sister's son - a boy of about your own age. I think he is making a mistake in leaving the factory, and going into the office. He will have little to do, and that not of a character to give him knowledge of business."

"Still, if he takes lessons in bookkeeping -"

Mr. Jennings smiled.

"The boy will never make a bookkeeper," he said. "His reason for desiring the change is because he is indolent. The world has no room for lazy people."

"I wonder, sir, that you have had a chance to find him out."

"Little things betray a boy's nature, or a man's, for that

matter. When I have visited the workroom I have noticed Leonard, and formed my conclusions. He is not a boy whom I would select for my service, but I have taken him as a favor to his uncle. I presume he is without means, and it is desirable that he should pay his uncle something in return for the home which he gives him."

"How much do you pay him, sir, if it is not a secret?"

"Oh, no; he receives five dollars a week to begin with. I will pay him the same in the office. And that reminds me; how would you like to have a situation in the factory? Would you like to take Leonard's place?"

"Yes, sir, if you think I would do."

"I feel quite sure of it. Have you ever done any manual labor?"

"No, sir."

"I suppose you have always been to school."

"Yes, sir."

"You are a gentleman's son," proceeded Mr. Jennings, eying Carl attentively. "How will it suit you to become a working boy?"

"I shall like it," answered Carl, promptly.

"Don't be too sure! You can tell better after a week in the factory. Those in my employ work ten hours a day. Leonard Craig doesn't like it."

"All I ask, Mr. Jennings, is that you give me a trial."

"That is fair," responded the little man, looking pleased. "I will tell you now that, not knowing of any vacancy in the factory, I had intended to give you the place in the office which Mr. Gibbon has asked for his nephew. It would have been a good deal easier work."

"I shall be quite satisfied to take my place in the factory."

"Come in, then, and see your future scene of employment."

They entered a large room, occupying nearly an entire floor of the building. Part of the space was filled by machinery. The number employed Carl estimated roughly at twenty-five.

Quite near the door was a boy, who bore some personal resemblance to the bookkeeper. Carl concluded that it must be Leonard Craig. The boy looked round as Mr. Jennings entered, and eyed Carl sharply.

"How are you getting on, Leonard?" Mr. Jennings asked.

"Pretty well, sir; but the machinery makes my head ache."

"Your uncle tells me that your employment does not agree with you."

"No, sir; I don't think it does."

"He would like to have you in the office with him.

Would you like it, also?"

"Yes, sir," answered Leonard, eagerly.

"Very well. You may report for duty at the office to-morrow morning. This boy will take your place here."

Leonard eyed Carl curiously, not cordially.

"I hope you'll like it," he said.

"I think I shall."

"You two boys must get acquainted," said Mr. Jennings. "Leonard, this is Carl Crawford."

"Glad to know you," said Leonard, coldly.

"I don't think I shall like that boy," thought Carl, as he followed Mr. Jennings to another part of the room.

CHAPTER XVII.

CARL ENTERS THE FACTORY.

When they left the factory Mr. Jennings said, with a smile:

"Now you are one of us, Carl. To-morrow you begin work."

"I am glad of it, sir."

"You don't ask what salary you are to get."

"I am willing to leave that to you."

"Suppose we say two dollars a week and board - to begin with."

"That is better than I expected. But where am I to board?"

"At my house, for the present, if that will suit you."

"I shall like it very much, if it won't inconvenience you."

"Hannah is the one to be inconvenienced, if anyone. I had a little conversation with her while you were getting ready for dinner. She seems to have taken a liking for you, though she doesn't like boys generally. As for me, it will make the home brighter to have a young person in it. Hannah and I are old-fashioned and quiet, and the neighbors don't have much reason to complain of noise."

"No, sir; I should think not, ' said Carl, with a smile.

"There is one thing you must be prepared for, Carl," said Mr. Jennings, after a pause.

"What is that, sir?"

"Your living in my house - I being your employer - may excite jealousy in some. I think I know of one who will be jealous."

"Leonard Craig?"

"And his uncle. However, don't borrow any trouble on that score. I hope you won't take advantage of your position, and, thinking yourself a favorite, neglect your duties."

"I will not, sir."

"Business and friendship ought to be kept apart."

"That is right, sir."

"I am going back to the house, but you may like to take a walk about the village. You will feel interested in it, as it is to be your future home. By the way, it may be well for you to write for your trunk. You can order it sent to my house."

"All right, sir; I will do so."

He went to the post office, and, buying a postal card, wrote to his friend, Gilbert Vance, as follows:

"Dear Gilbert: - Please send my trunk by express to me at Milford, care of Henry Jennings, Esq. He is my employer, and I live at his house. He is proprietor of a furniture factory. Will write further particulars soon.

"Carl Crawford."

This postal carried welcome intelligence to Gilbert, who felt a brotherly interest in Carl. He responded by a letter of hearty congratulation, and forwarded the trunk as requested.

Carl reported for duty the next morning, and, though a novice, soon showed that he was not without mechanical skill.

At twelve o'clock all the factory hands had an hour off for dinner. As Carl passed into the street he found himself walking beside the boy whom he had succeeded - Leonard Craig.

"Good-morning, Leonard," said Carl, pleasantly.

"Good-morning. Have you taken my place in the factory?"

"Yes."

"Do you think you shall like it?"

"I think I shall, though, of course, it is rather early to form an opinion."

"I didn't like it."

"Why not?"

"I don't want to grow up a workman. I think I am fit for something better."

"Mr. Jennings began as a factory hand."

"I suppose he had a taste for it. I haven't."

"Then you like your present position better?"

"Oh, yes; it's more genteel. How much does Jennings pay you?"

"Two dollars a week and board."

"How is that? Where do you board?"

"With him."

"Oh!" said Leonard, his countenance changing. "So you are a favorite with the boss, are you?"

"I don't know. He gave me warning that he should be just as strict with me as if we were strangers."

"How long have you known him?"

Carl smiled.

"I met him for the first time yesterday," he answered.

"That's very queer."

"Well, perhaps it is a little singular."

"Are you a poor boy?"

"I have to earn my own living."

"I see. You will grow up a common workman."

"I shall try to rise above it. I am not ashamed of the position, but I am ambitious to rise."

"I am going to be a bookkeeper," said Leonard. "My uncle is going to teach me. I would rather be a bookkeeper than a factory hand."

"Then you are right in preparing yourself for such a post."

Here the two boys separated, as they were to dine in different places.

Leonard was pleased with his new position. He really had very little to do. Twice a day he went to the post office, once or twice to the bank, and there was an occasional errand besides. To Carl the idleness would have been insupportable, but Leonard was naturally indolent. He sat down in a chair by the window, and watched the people go by.

The first afternoon he was in luck, for there was a dog fight in the street outside. He seized his hat, went out, and watched the canine warfare with the deepest interest.

"I think I will buy you a system of bookkeeping," said his uncle, "and you can study it in the office."

"Put it off till next week, Uncle Julius. I want to get rested from the factory work."

"It seems to me, Leonard, you were born lazy," said his uncle, sharply.

"I don't care to work with my hands."

"Do you care to work at all?"

"I should like to be a bookkeeper."

"Do you know that my work is harder and more exhausting than that of a workman in the factory?"

"You don't want to exchange with him, do you?" asked Leonard.

"No."

"That's where I agree with you."

Mr. Jennings took several weekly papers. Leonard was looking over the columns of one of them one day, when he saw the advertisement of a gift enterprise of a most attractive character. The first prize was a house and grounds valued at ten thousand dollars. Following were minor prizes, among them one thousand dollars in gold.

Leonard's fancy was captivated by the brilliant prospect of such a prize.

"Price of tickets - only one dollar!" he read. "Think of getting a thousand dollars for one! Oh, if I could only be the lucky one!"

He took out his purse, though he knew beforehand that his stock of cash consisted only of two dimes and a nickel.

"I wonder if I could borrow a dollar of that boy Carl!" he deliberated. "I'll speak to him about it."

This happened more than a week after Carl went to work in the factory. He had already received one week's pay, and it remained untouched in his pocket.

Leonard joined him in the street early in the evening, and accosted him graciously.

"Where are you going?" he asked.

"Nowhere in particular. I am out for a walk."

"So am I. Shall we walk together?"

"If you like."

After talking on indifferent matters, Leonard said suddenly: "Oh, by the way, will you do me a favor?"

"What is it?"

"Lend me a dollar till next week."

In former days Carl would probably have granted the favor, but he realized the value of money now that he had to earn it by steady work.

"I am afraid it won't be convenient," he answered.

"Does that mean that you haven't got it?" asked Leonard.

"No, I have it, but I am expecting to use it."

"I wouldn't mind paying you interest for it - say twenty-five cents," continued Leonard, who had set his heart on buying a ticket in the gift enterprise.

"I would be ashamed to take such interest as that."

"But I have a chance of making a good deal more out of it myself."

"In what way?"

"That is my secret."

"Why don't you borrow it of your uncle?"

"He would ask too many questions. However, I see that you're a miser, and I won't trouble you."

He left Carl in a huff and walked hastily away. He turned into a lane little traveled, and, after walking a few rods, came suddenly upon the prostrate body of a man, whose deep, breathing showed that he was stupefied by liquor. Leonard was not likely to feel any special interest in him, but one object did attract his attention. It was a wallet which had dropped out of the man's pocket and was lying on the grass beside him.

CHAPTER XVIII.

LEONARD'S TEMPTATION.

Leonard was not a thief, but the sight of the wallet tempted him, under the circumstances. He had set his heart on buying a ticket in the gift enterprise, and knew of no way of obtaining the requisite sum - except this. It was, indeed, a little shock to him to think of appropriating money not his own; yet who would know it? The owner of the wallet was drunk, and would be quite unconscious of his loss. Besides, if he didn't take the wallet, some one else probably would, and appropriate the entire contents. It was an insidious suggestion, and Leonard somehow persuaded himself that since the money was sure to be taken, he might as well have the benefit of it as anyone else.

So, after turning over the matter in his mind rapidly, he stooped down and picked up the wallet.

The man did not move.

Emboldened by his insensibility, Leonard cautiously opened the pocketbook, and his eyes glistened when he saw tucked away in one side, quite a thick roll of bills.

"He won't miss one bill," thought Leonard. "Anyone else might take the whole wallet, but I wouldn't do that. I wonder how much money there is in the roll."

He darted another glance at the prostrate form, but there seemed no danger of interruption. He took the roll in his hand, therefore, and a hasty scrutiny showed him that the bills ran from ones to tens. There must have been nearly a hundred dollars in all.

"Suppose I take a five," thought Leonard, whose cupidity increased with the sight of the money. "He won't miss it, and it will be better in my hands than if spent for whiskey."

How specious are the arguments of those who seek an excuse for a wrong act that will put money in the purse!

"Yes, I think I may venture to take a five, and, as I might not be able to change it right away, I will take a one to send for a ticket. Then I will put the wallet back in the man's pocket."

So far, all went smoothly, and Leonard was proceeding to carry out his intention when, taking a precautionary look at the man on the ground, he was dumfounded by seeing his eyes wide open and fixed upon him.

Leonard flushed painfully, like a criminal detected in a crime, and returned the look of inquiry by one of dismay.

"What - you - doing?" inquired the victim of inebriety.

"I - is this your wallet, sir?" stammered Leonard.

"Course it is. What you got it for?"

"I - I saw it on the ground, and was afraid some one would find it, and rob you," said Leonard, fluently.

"Somebody did find it," rejoined the man, whose senses seemed coming back to him. "How much did you take?"

"I? You don't think I would take any of your money?" said Leonard, in virtuous surprise.

"Looked like it! Can't tell who to trust."

"I assure you, I had only just picked it up, and was going to put it back in your pocket, sir."

The man, drunk as he was, winked knowingly.

"Smart boy!" he said. "You do it well, ol' fella!"

"But, sir, it is quite true, I assure you. I will count over the money before you. Do you know how much you had?"

"Nev' mind. Help me up!"

Leonard stooped over and helped the drunkard to a sitting position.

"Where am I? Where is hotel?"

Leonard answered him.

"Take me to hotel, and I'll give you a dollar."

"Certainly, sir," said Leonard, briskly. He was to get his dollar after all, and would not have to steal it. I am afraid he is not to be praised for his honesty, as it seemed to be a matter of necessity.

"I wish he'd give me five dollars," thought Leonard, but didn't see his way clear to make the suggestion.

He placed the man on his feet, and guided his steps to the road. As he walked along, the inebriate, whose gait was at first unsteady, recovered his equilibrium and required less help.

"How long had you been lying there?" asked Leonard.

"Don't know. I was taken sick," and the inebriate nodded knowingly at Leonard, who felt at liberty to laugh, too.

"Do you ever get sick?"

"Not that way," answered Leonard.

"Smart boy! Better off!"

They reached the hotel, and Leonard engaged a room for his companion.

"Has he got money?" asked the landlord, in a low voice.

"Yes," answered Leonard, "he has nearly a hundred dollars. I counted it myself."

"That's all right, then," said the landlord. "Here, James, show the gentleman up to No. 15."

"Come, too," said the stranger to Leonard.

The latter followed the more readily because he had not yet been paid his dollar.

The door of No. 15 was opened, and the two entered.

"I will stay with the gentleman a short time," said Leonard to the boy. "If we want anything we will ring."

"All right, sir."

"What's your name?" asked the inebriate, as he sank into a large armchair near the window.

"Leonard Craig."

"Never heard the name before."

"What's your name, sir?"

"What yon want to know for?" asked the other, cunningly.

"The landlord will want to put it on his book."

"My name? Phil Stark."

"Philip Stark?"

"Yes; who told you?"

It will be seen that Mr. Stark was not yet quite himself.

"You told me yourself."

"So I did - 'scuse me."

"Certainly, sir. By the way, you told me you would pay me a dollar for bringing you to the hotel."

"So I did. Take it," and Philip Stark passed the wallet to Leonard.

Leonard felt tempted to take a two-dollar bill instead of a one, as Mr. Stark would hardly notice the mistake. Still, he might ask to look at the bill, and that would be awkward. So the boy contented himself with the sum promised.

"Thank you, sir," he said, as he slipped the bill into his vest pocket. "Do you want some supper?"

"No, I want to sleep."

"Then you had better lie down on the bed. Will you undress?"

"No; too much trouble."

Mr. Stark rose from the armchair, and, lurching round to the bed, flung himself on it.

"I suppose you don't want me any longer," said Leonard.

"No. Come round to-morrer."

"Yes, sir."

Leonard opened the door and left the room. He resolved to keep the appointment, and come round the next day. Who knew but some more of Mr. Stark's money might come into his hands? Grown man as he was, he seemed to need a guardian, and Leonard was willing to act as such - for a consideration.

"It's been a queer adventure!" thought Leonard, as he slowly bent his steps towards his uncle's house. "I've made a dollar out of it, anyway, and if he hadn't happened to wake up just as he did I might have done better. However, it may turn out as well in the end."

"You are rather late, Leonard," said his uncle, in a tone that betrayed some irritation. "I wanted to send you on an errand, and you are always out of the way at such a time."

"I'll go now," said Leonard, with unusual amiability. "I've had a little adventure."

"An adventure! What is it?" Mr. Gibbon asked, with curiosity.

Leonard proceeded to give an account of his finding the inebriate in the meadow, and his guiding him to the hotel. It may readily be supposed that he said nothing of his attempt to appropriate a part of the contents of the wallet.

"What was his name?" asked Gibbon, with languid curiosity.

"Phil Stark, he calls himself."

A strange change came over the face of the book-keeper. There was a frightened look in his eyes, and his color faded.

"Phil Stark!" he repeated, in a startled tone.

"Yes, sir."

"What brings him here?" Gibbon asked himself nervously, but no words passed his lips.

"Do you know the name?" asked Leonard, wonderingly.

"I - have heard it before, but - no, I don't think it is the same man."

CHAPTER XIX.

AN ARTFUL SCHEME.

"Does this Mr. Stark intend to remain long in the village!" inquired the bookkeeper, in a tone of assumed indifference.

"He didn't say anything on that point," answered Leonard.

"He did not say what business brought him here, I presume?"

"No, he was hardly in condition to say much; he was pretty full," said Leonard, with a laugh. "However, he wants me to call upon him to-morrow, and may tell me then."

"He wants you to call upon him?"

"Yes, uncle."

"Are you going?"

"Yes; why shouldn't I?"

"I see no reason," said Gibbon, hesitating. Then, after a pause he added: "If you see the way clear, find out what brings him to Milford."

"Yes, uncle, I will."

"Uncle Julius seems a good deal interested in this man, considering that he is a stranger," thought the boy.

The bookkeeper was biting his nails, a habit he had when he was annoyed. "And, Leonard," he added slowly, "don't mention my name while you are speaking to Stark."

"No, sir, I won't, if you don't want me to," answered Leonard, his face betraying unmistakable curiosity. His uncle noted this, and explained hurriedly: "It is possible that he may be a man whom I once met under disagreeable circumstances, and I would prefer not to meet him again. Should he learn that I was living here, he would be sure to want to renew the acquaintance."

"Yes, sir, I see. I don't think he would want to borrow money, for he seems to be pretty well provided. I made a dollar out of him to-day, and that is one reason why I am willing to call on him again. I may strike him for another bill."

"There is no objection to that, provided you don't talk to him too freely. I don't think he will want to stay long in Milford."

"I wouldn't if I had as much money as he probably has."

"Do you often meet the new boy?"

"Carl Crawford?"

Horatio Alger, Jr.

"Yes; I see him on the street quite often."

"He lives with Mr. Jennings, I hear."

"So he tells me."

"It is rather strange. I didn't suppose that Jennings would care to receive a boy in his house, or that tall grenadier of a housekeeper, either. I expect she rules the household."

"She could tuck him under her arm and walk off with him," said Leonard, laughing.

"The boy must be artful to have wormed his way into the favor of the strange pair. He seems to be a favorite."

"Yes, uncle, I think he is. However, I like my position better than his."

"He will learn his business from the beginning. I don't know but it was a mistake for you to leave the factory."

"I am not at all sorry for it, uncle."

"Your position doesn't amount to much."

"I am paid just as well as I was when I was in the factory."

"But you are learning nothing."

"You are going to teach me bookkeeping."

"Even that is not altogether a desirable business. A

good bookkeeper can never expect to be in business for himself. He must be content with a salary all his life."

"You have done pretty well, uncle."

"But there is no chance of my becoming a rich man. I have to work hard for my money. And I haven't been able to lay up much money yet. That reminds me? Leonard, I must impress upon you the fact that you have your own way to make. I have procured you a place, and I provide you a home -"

"You take my wages," said Leonard, bluntly.

"A part of them, but on the whole, you are not self-supporting. You must look ahead, Leonard, and consider the future. When you are a young man you will want to earn an adequate income."

"Of course, I shall, uncle, but there is one other course."

"What is that?"

"I may marry an heiress," suggested Leonard, smiling.

The bookkeeper winced.

"I thought I was marrying an heiress when I married your aunt," he said, "but within six months of our wedding day, her father made a bad failure, and actually had the assurance to ask me to give him a home under my roof."

"Did you do it?"

"No; I told him it would not be convenient."

"What became of him?"

"He got a small clerkship at ten dollars a week in the counting room of a mercantile friend, and filled it till one day last October, when he dropped dead of apoplexy. I made a great mistake when I married in not asking him to settle a definite sum on his daughter. It would have been so much saved from the wreck."

"Did aunt want him to come and live here?"

"Yes, women are always unreasonable. She would have had me support the old man in idleness, but I am not one of that kind. Every tub should stand on its own bottom."

"I say so, too, uncle. Do you know whether this boy, Carl Crawford, has any father or mother?"

"From a word Jennings let fall I infer that he has relatives, but is not on good terms with them. I have been a little afraid he might stand in your light."

"How so, uncle?"

"Should there be any good opening for one of your age, I am afraid he would get it rather than you."

"I didn't think of that," said Leonard, jealously.

"Living as he does with Mr. Jennings, he will naturally try to ingratiate himself with him, and stand first in his esteem."

"That is true. Is Mr. Jennings a rich man, do you think?"

"Yes, I think he is. The factory and stock are worth considerable money, but I know he has other investments also. As one item he has over a thousand dollars in the Carterville Savings Bank. He has been very prudent, has met with no losses, and has put aside a great share of his profits every year."

"I wonder he don't marry."

"Marriage doesn't seem to be in his thoughts. Hannah makes him so comfortable that he will probably remain a bachelor to the end of his days."

"Perhaps he will leave his money to her."

"He is likely to live as long as she."

"She is a good deal longer than he," said Leonard, with a laugh.

The bookkeeper condescended to smile at this joke, though it was not very brilliant.

"Before this boy Carl came," he resumed thoughtfully, "I hoped he might take a fancy to you. He must die some time, and, having no near blood relative, I thought he might select as heir some boy like yourself, who might grow into his favor and get on his blind side."

"Is it too late now?" asked Leonard, eagerly.

"Perhaps not, but the appearance of this new boy on

the scene makes your chance a good deal smaller."

"I wish we could get rid of him," said Leonard, frowning.

"The only way is to injure him in the estimation of Mr. Jennings."

"I think I know of a way."

"Mention it."

"Here is an advertisement of a lottery," said Leonard, whose plans, in view of what his uncle had said, had experienced a change.

"Well?"

"I will write to the manager in Carl's name, inquiring about tickets, and, of course, he will answer to him, to the care of Mr. Jennings. This will lead to the suspicion that Carl is interested in such matters."

"It is a good idea. It will open the way to a loss of confidence on the part of Mr. Jennings."

"I will sit down at your desk and write at once."

Three days later Mr. Jennings handed a letter to Carl after they reached home in the evening.

"A letter for you to my care," he explained.

Carl opened it in surprise, and read as follows:

"Office Of Gift Enterprise.

"Mr. Carl Crawford: - Your letter of inquiry is received. In reply we would say that we will send you six tickets for five dollars. By disposing of them among your friends at one dollar each, you will save the cost of your own. You had better remit at once.

"Yours respectfully, Pitkins & Gamp,

"Agents."

Carl looked the picture of astonishment when he read this letter.

CHAPTER XX.

REVEALS A MYSTERY.

"Please read this letter, Mr. Jennings," said Carl.

His employer took the letter from his hand, and ran his eye over it.

"Do you wish to ask my advice about the investment?" he said, quietly.

"No, sir. I wanted to know how such a letter came to be written to me."

"Didn't you send a letter of inquiry there?"

"No, sir, and I can't understand how these men could have got hold of my name."

Mr. Jennings looked thoughtful.

"Some one has probably written in your name," he said, after a pause.

"But who could have done so?"

"If you will leave the letter in my hands, I may be able to obtain some information on that point."

"I shall be glad if you can, Mr. Jennings."

"Don't mention to anyone having received such a letter, and if anyone broaches the subject, let me know who it is."

"Yes, sir, I will."

Mr. Jennings quietly put on his hat, and walked over to the post office. The postmaster, who also kept a general variety store, chanced to be alone.

"Good-evening, Mr. Jennings," he said, pleasantly. "What can I do for you?"

"I want a little information, Mr. Sweetland, though it is doubtful if you can give it."

Mr. Sweetland assumed the attitude of attention.

"Do you know if any letter has been posted from this office within a few days, addressed to Pitkins & Gamp, Syracuse, New York?"

"Yes; two letters have been handed in bearing this address."

Mr. Jennings was surprised, for he had never thought of two letters.

"Can you tell me who handed them in?" he asked.

"Both were handed in by the same party."

"And that was -"

"A boy in your employ."

Mr. Jennings looked grave. Was it possible that Carl was deceiving him?

"The boy who lives at my house?" he asked, anxiously.

"No; the boy who usually calls for the factory mail. The nephew of your bookkeeper I think his name is Leonard Craig."

"Ah, I see," said Mr. Jennings, looking very much relieved. "And you say he deposited both letters?"

"Yes, sir."

"Do you happen to remember if any other letter like this was received at the office?"

Here he displayed the envelope of Carl's letter.

"Yes; one was received, addressed to the name of the one who deposited the first letters -
Leonard Craig."

"Thank you, Mr. Sweetland. Your information has cleared up a mystery. Be kind enough not to mention the matter."

"I will bear your request in mind."

Mr. Jennings bought a supply of stamps, and then left the office.

"Well, Carl," he said, when he re-entered the house, "I have discovered who wrote in your name to Pitkins

& Gamp."

"Who, sir?" asked Carl, with curiosity.

"Leonard Craig."

"But what could induce him to do it?" said Carl, perplexed.

"He thought that I would see the letter, and would be prejudiced against you if I discovered that you were investing in what is a species of lottery."

"Would you, sir?"

"I should have thought you unwise, and I should have been reminded of a fellow workman who became so infatuated with lotteries that he stole money from his employer to enable him to continue his purchases of tickets. But for this unhappy passion he would have remained honest."

"Leonard must dislike me," said Carl, thoughtfully.

"He is jealous of you; I warned you he or some one else might become so. But the most curious circumstance is, he wrote a second letter in his own name. I suspect he has bought a ticket. I advise you to say nothing about the matter unless questioned."

"I won't, sir."

The next day Carl met Leonard in the street.

"By the way," said Leonard, "you got a letter yesterday?"

"Yes."

"I brought it to the factory with the rest of the mail."

"Thank you."

Leonard looked at him curiously.

"He seems to be close-mouthed," Leonard said to himself. "He has sent for a ticket, I'll bet a hat, and don't want me to find out. I wish I could draw the capital prize - I would not mind old Jennings finding out then."

"Do you ever hear from your - friends?" he asked a minute later.

"Not often."

"I thought that letter might be from your home."

"No; it was a letter from Syracuse."

"I remember now, it was postmarked Syracuse. Have you friends there?"

"None that I am aware of."

"Yet you receive letters from there?"

"That was a business letter."

Carl was quietly amused at Leonard's skillful questions, but was determined not to give him any light on the subject.

Leonard tried another avenue of attack.

"Oh, dear!" he sighed, "I wish I was rich."

"I shouldn't mind being rich myself," said Carl, with a smile.

"I suppose old Jennings must have a lot of money."

"Mr. Jennings, I presume, is very well off," responded Carl, emphasizing the title "Mr."

"If I had his money I wouldn't live in such Quaker style."

"Would you have him give fashionable parties?" asked Carl, smiling.

"Well, I don't know that he would enjoy that; but I'll tell you what I would do. I would buy a fast horse - a two-forty mare - and a bangup buggy, and I'd show the old farmers round here what fast driving is. Then I'd have a stylish house, and -"

"I don't believe you'd be content to live in Milford, Leonard."

"I don't think I would, either, unless my business were here. I'd go to New York every few weeks and see life."

"You may be rich some time, so that you can carry out your wishes."

"Do you know any easy way of getting money?" asked Leonard, pointedly.

"The easy ways are not generally the true ways. A man sometimes makes money by speculation, but he has to have some to begin with."

"I can't get anything out of him," thought Leonard. "Well, good-evening."

He crossed the street, and joined the man who has already been referred to as boarding at the hotel.

Mr. Stark had now been several days in Milford. What brought him there, or what object he had in staying, Leonard had not yet ascertained. He generally spent part of his evenings with the stranger, and had once or twice received from him a small sum of money. Usually, however, he had met Mr. Stark in the billiard room, and played a game or two of billiards with him. Mr. Stark always paid for the use of the table, and that was naturally satisfactory to Leonard, who enjoyed amusement at the expense of others.

Leonard, bearing in mind his uncle's request, had not mentioned his name to Mr. Stark, and Stark, though he had walked about the village more or less, had not chanced to meet Mr. Gibbon.

He had questioned Leonard, however, about Mr. Jennings, and whether he was supposed to be rich.

Leonard had answered freely that everyone considered him so.

"But he doesn't know how to enjoy his money," he added.

"We should," said Stark, jocularly.

"You bet we would," returned Leonard; and he was quite sincere in his boast, as we know from his conversation with Carl.

"By the way," said Stark, on this particular evening, "I never asked you about your family, Leonard. I suppose you live with your parents."

"No, sir. They are dead."

"Then whom do you live with?"

"With my uncle," answered Leonard, guardedly.

"Is his name Craig?"

"No."

"What then?"

"I've got to tell him," thought Leonard. "Well, I don't suppose there will be much harm in it. My uncle is bookkeeper for Mr. Jennings," he said, "and his name is Julius Gibbon."

Philip Stark wheeled round, and eyed Leonard in blank astonishment.

"Your uncle is Julius Gibbon!" he exclaimed.

"Yes."

"Well, I'll be blowed."

"Do you - know my uncle?" asked Leonard, hesitating.

"I rather think I do. Take me round to the house. I want to see him."

CHAPTER XXI.

AN UNWELCOME GUEST.

When Julius Gibbon saw the door open and Philip Stark enter the room where he was smoking his noon cigar, his heart quickened its pulsations and he turned pale.

"How are you, old friend?" said Stark, boisterously. "Funny, isn't it, that I should run across your nephew?"

"Very strange!" ejaculated Gibbon, looking the reverse of joyous.

"It's a happy meeting, isn't it? We used to see a good deal of each other," and he laughed in a way that Gibbon was far from enjoying. "Now, I've come over to have a good, long chat with you. Leonard, I think we won't keep you, as you wouldn't be interested in our talk about old times."

"Yes, Leonard, you may leave us," added his uncle.

Leonard's curiosity was excited, and he would have been glad to remain, but as there was no help for it, he went out.

When they were alone, Stark drew up his chair close,

Horatio Alger, Jr.

and laid his hand familiarly on the bookkeeper's knee.

"I say, Gibbon, do you remember where we last met?"

Gibbon shuddered slightly.

"Yes," he answered, feebly.

"It was at Joliet - Joliet Penitentiary. Your time expired before mine. I envied you the six months' advantage you had of me. When I came out I searched for you everywhere, but heard nothing."

"How did you know I was here?" asked the bookkeeper.

"I didn't know. I had no suspicion of it. Nor did I dream that Leonard, who was able to do me a little service, was your nephew. I say, he's a chip of the old block, Gibbon," and Stark laughed as if he enjoyed it.

"What do you mean by that?"

"I was lying in a field, overcome by liquor, an old weakness of mine, you know, and my wallet had slipped out of my pocket. I chanced to open my eyes, when I saw it in the hands of your promising nephew, ha! ha!"

"He told me that."

"But he didn't tell you that he was on the point of appropriating a part of the contents? I warrant you he didn't tell you that."

"Did he acknowledge it? Perhaps you misjudged him."

"He didn't acknowledge it in so many words, but I knew it by his change of color and confusion. Oh, I didn't lay it up against him. We are very good friends. He comes honestly by it."

Gibbon looked very much annoyed, but there were reasons why he did not care to express his chagrin.

"On my honor, it was an immense surprise to me," proceeded Stark, "when I learned that my old friend Gibbon was a resident of Milford."

"I wish you had never found it out," thought Gibbon, biting his lip.

"No sooner did I hear it than I posted off at once to call on you."

"So I see."

Stark elevated his eyebrows, and looked amused. He saw that he was not a welcome visitor, but for that he cared little.

"Haven't you got on, though? Here I find you the trusted bookkeeper of an important business firm. Did you bring recommendations from your last place?" and he burst into a loud guffaw.

"I wish you wouldn't make such references," snapped Gibbon. "They can do no good, and might do harm."

"Don't be angry, my dear boy. I rejoice at your good fortune. Wish I was equally well fixed. You don't ask how I am getting on."

"I hope you are prosperous," said Gibbon, coldly.

"I might be more so. Is there a place vacant in your office?"

"No."

"And if there were, you might not recommend me, eh?"

"There is no need to speak of that. There is no vacancy."

"Upon my word, I wish there were, as I am getting to the end of my tether. I may have money enough to last me four weeks longer, but no more."

"I don't see how I can help you," said Gibbon.

"How much salary does Mr. Jennings pay you?"

"A hundred dollars a month," answered the book-keeper, reluctantly.

"Not bad, in a cheap place like this."

"It takes all I make to pay expenses."

"I remember - you have a wife. I have no such incumbrance."

"There is one question I would like to ask you," said the bookkeeper.

"Fire away, dear boy. Have you an extra cigar?"

"Here is one,"

"Thanks. Now I shall be comfortable. Go ahead with your question."

"What brought you to Milford? You didn't know of my being here, you say."

"Neither did I. I came on my old business."

"What?"

"I heard there was a rich manufacturer here - I allude to your respected employer. I thought I might manage to open his safe some dark night."

"No, no," protested Gibbon in alarm. "Don't think of it."

"Why not?" asked Stark, coolly.

"Because," answered Gibbon, in some agitation, "I might be suspected."

"Well, perhaps you might; but I have got to look out for number one. How do you expect me to live?"

"Go somewhere else. There are plenty of other men as rich, and richer, where you would not be compromising an old friend."

"It's because I have an old friend in the office that I have thought this would be my best opening."

"Surely, man, you don't expect me to betray my employer, and join with you in robbing him?"

"That's just what I do expect. Don't tell me you have grown virtuous, Gibbon. The tiger doesn't lose his spots or the leopard his stripes. I tell you there's a fine chance for us both. I'll divide with you, if you'll help me."

"But I've gone out of the business," protested Gibbon.

"I haven't. Come, old boy, I can't let any sentimental scruples interfere with so good a stroke of business."

"I won't help you!" said Gibbon, angrily. "You only want to get me into trouble."

"You won't help me?" said Stark, with slow deliberation.

"No, I can't honorably. Can't you let me alone?"

"Sorry to say, I can't. If I was rich, I might; but as it is, it is quite necessary for me to raise some money somewhere. By all accounts, Jennings is rich, and can spare a small part of his accumulations for a good fellow that's out of luck."

"You'd better give up the idea. It's quite impossible."

"Is it?" asked Stark, with a wicked look. "Then do you know what I will do?"

"What will you do?" asked Gibbon, nervously.

"I will call on your employer, and tell him what I know of you."

"You wouldn't do that?" said the bookkeeper,

much agitated.

"Why not? You turn your back upon an old friend. You bask in prosperity, and turn from him in his poverty. It's the way of the world, no doubt; but Phil Stark generally gets even with those who don't treat him well."

"Tell me what you want me to do," said Gibbon, desperately.

"Tell me first whether your safe contains much of value."

"We keep a line of deposit with the Milford Bank."

"Do you mean to say that nothing of value is left in the safe overnight?" asked Stark, disappointed

"There is a box of government bonds usually kept there," the bookkeeper admitted, reluctantly.

"Ah, that's good!" returned Stark, rubbing his hands. "Do you know how much they amount to?"

"I think there are about four thousand dollars."

"Good! We must have those bonds, Gibbon."

CHAPTER XXII.

MR. STARK IS RECOGNIZED.

Phil Stark was resolved not to release his hold upon his old acquaintance. During the day he spent his time in lounging about the town, but in the evening he invariably fetched up at the bookkeeper's modest home. His attentions were evidently not welcome to Mr. Gibbon, who daily grew more and more nervous and irritable, and had the appearance of a man whom something disquieted.

Leonard watched the growing intimacy with curiosity. He was a sharp boy, and he felt convinced that there was something between his uncle and the stranger. There was no chance for him to overhear any conversation, for he was always sent out of the way when the two were closeted together. He still met Mr. Stark outside, and played billiards with him frequently. Once he tried to extract some information from Stark.

"You've known my uncle a good while," he said, in a tone of assumed indifference.

"Yes, a good many years," answered Stark, as he made a carom.

"Were you in business together?"

"Not exactly, but we may be some time," returned Stark, with a significant smile.

"Here?"

"Well, that isn't decided."

"Where did you first meet Uncle Julius?"

"The kid's growing curious," said Stark to himself. "Does he think he can pull wool over the eyes of Phil Stark? If he does, he thinks a good deal too highly of himself. I will answer his questions to suit myself."

"Why don't you ask your uncle that?"

"I did," said Leonard, "but he snapped me up, and told me to mind my own business. He is getting terribly cross lately."

"It's his stomach, I presume," said Stark, urbanely. "He is a confirmed dyspeptic - that's what's the matter with him. Now; I've got the digestion of an ox. Nothing ever troubles me, and the result is that I am as calm and good-natured as a May morning."

"Don't you ever get riled, Mr. Stark?" asked Leonard, laughing.

"Well, hardly ever. Sometimes when I am asked fool questions by one who seems to be prying into what is none of his business, I get wrathy, and when I'm roused look out !"

He glanced meaningly at Leonard, and the boy understood that the words conveyed a warning and a menace.

"Is anything the matter with you, Mr. Gibbon? Are you as well as usual?" asked Mr. Jennings one morning. The little man was always considerate, and he had noticed the flurried and nervous manner of his bookkeeper.

"No, sir; what makes you ask?" said Gibbon, apologetically.

"Perhaps you need a vacation," suggested Mr. Jennings.

"Oh, no, I think not. Besides, I couldn't be spared."

"I would keep the books myself for a week to favor you."

"You are very kind, but I won't trouble you just yet. A little later on, if I feel more uncomfortable, I will avail myself of your kindness."

"Do so. I know that bookkeeping is a strain upon the mind, more so than physical labor."

There were special reasons why Mr. Gibbon did not dare to accept the vacation tendered him by his employer. He knew that Phil Stark would be furious, for it would interfere with his designs. He could not afford to offend this man, who held in his possession a secret affecting his reputation and good name.

The presence of a stranger in a small town always attracts public attention, and many were curious about the rakish-looking man who had now for some time occupied a room at the hotel.

Among others, Carl had several times seen him walking with Leonard Craig

"Leonard," he asked one day, "who is the gentleman I see you so often walking with?"

"It's a man that's boarding at the hotel. I play billiards with him sometimes."

"He seems to like Milford."

"I don't know. He's over at our house every evening."

"Is he?" asked Carl, surprised.

"Yes; he's an old acquaintance of Uncle Julius. I don't know where they met each other, for he won't tell. He said he and uncle might go into business together some time. Between you and me, I think uncle would like to get rid of him. I know he doesn't like him."

This set Carl to thinking, but something occurred soon afterwards that impressed him still more.

Occasionally a customer of the house visited Milford, wishing to give a special order for some particular line of goods. About this time a Mr. Thorndike, from Chicago, came to Milford on this errand, and put up at the hotel. He had called at the factory during the day, and had some conversation with Mr. Jennings. After supper a doubt entered the mind of the manufacturer in regard to one point, and he said to Carl: "Carl, are you engaged this evening?"

"No, sir."

"Will you carry a note for me to the hotel?"

"Certainly, sir; I shall be glad to do so."

"Mr. Thorndike leaves in the morning, and I am not quite clear as to one of the specifications he gave me with his order. You noticed the gentleman who went through the factory with me?"

"Yes, sir."

"He is Mr. Thorndike. Please hand him this note, and if he wishes you to remain with him for company, you had better do so."

"I will, sir."

"Hannah," said Mr. Jennings, as his messenger left with the note, "Carl is a pleasant addition to our little household?"

"Yes, indeed he is," responded Hannah, emphatically.

"If he was twice the trouble I'd be glad to have him here."

"He is easy to get along with."

"Surely."

"Yet his stepmother drove him from his father's house."

"She's a wicked trollop, then!" said Hannah, in a deep,

stern voice. "I'd like to get hold of her, I would."

"What would you do to her?" asked Mr. Jennings, smiling.

"I'd give her a good shaking," answered Hannah.

"I believe you would, Hannah," said Mr. Jennings, amused. "On the whole, I think she had better keep out of your clutches. Still, but for her we would never have met with Carl. What is his father's loss is our gain."

"What a poor, weak man his father must be," said Hannah, contemptuously, "to let a woman like her turn him against his own flesh and blood!"

"I agree with you, Hannah. I hope some time he may see his mistake."

Carl kept on his way to the hotel. It was summer and Mr. Thorndike was sitting on the piazza smoking a cigar. To him Carl delivered the note.

"It's all right!" he said, rapidly glancing it over. "You may tell Mr. Jennings," and here he gave an answer to the question asked in the letter.

"Yes, sir, I will remember."

"Won't you sit down and keep me company a little while?" asked Thorndike, who was sociably inclined.

"Thank you, sir," and Carl sat down in a chair beside him.

"Will you have a cigar?"

"No, thank you, sir. I don't smoke."

"That is where you are sensible. I began to smoke at fourteen, and now I find it hard to break off. My doctor tells me it is hurting me, but the chains of habit are strong."

"All the more reason for forming good habits, sir."

"Spoken like a philosopher. Are you in the employ of my friend, Mr. Jennings?"

"Yes, sir."

"Learning the business?"

"That is my present intention."

"If you ever come out to Chicago, call on me, and if you are out of a place, I will give you one."

"Are you not a little rash, Mr. Thorndike, to offer me a place when you know so little of me?"

"I trust a good deal to looks. I care more for them than for recommendations."

At that moment Phil Stark came out of the hotel, and passing them, stepped off the piazza into the street.

Mr. Thorndike half rose from his seat, and looked after him.

"Who is that?" he asked, in an exciting whisper.

"A man named Stark, who is boarding at the hotel. Do

you know him?"

"Do I know him?" repeated Thorndike. "He is one of the most successful burglars in the West."

CHAPTER XXIII.

PREPARING FOR THE BURGLAR.

Carl stared at Mr. Thorndike in surprise and dismay.

"A burglar!" he ejaculated.

"Yes; I was present in the courtroom when he was convicted of robbing the Springfield bank. I sat there for three hours, and his face was impressed upon my memory. I saw him later on in the Joliet Penitentiary. I was visiting the institution and saw the prisoners file out into the yard. I recognized this man instantly. Do you know how long he has been here?"

"For two weeks I should think."

"He has some dishonest scheme in his head, I have no doubt. Have you a bank in Milford?"

"Yes."

"He may have some design upon that."

"He is very intimate with our bookkeeper, so his nephew tells me."

Mr. Thorndike looked startled.

"Ha! I scent danger to my friend, Mr. Jennings. He ought to be apprised."

"He shall be, sir," said Carl, firmly.

"Will you see him to-night?"

"Yes, sir; I am not only in his employ, but I live at his house."

"That is well."

"Perhaps I ought to go home at once."

"No attempt will be made to rob the office till late. It is scarcely eight o'clock. I don't know, however, but I will walk around to the house with you, and tell your employer what I know. By the way, what sort of a man is the bookkeeper?"

"I don't know him very well, sir. He has a nephew in the office, who was transferred from the factory. I have taken his place."

"Do you think the bookkeeper would join in a plot to rob his employer?"

"I don't like him. To me he is always disagreeable, but I would not like to say that."

"How long has he been in the employ of Mr. Jennings?"

"As long as two years, I should think."

"You say that this man is intimate with him?"

"Leonard Craig - he is the nephew - says that Mr. Philip Stark is at his uncle's house every evening."

"So he calls himself Philip Stark, does he?"

"Isn't that his name?"

"I suppose it is one of his names. He was convicted under that name, and retains it here on account of its being so far from the place of his conviction. Whether it is his real name or not, I do not know. What is the name of your bookkeeper?"

"Julius Gibbon."

"I don't remember ever having heard it. Evidently there has been some past acquaintance between the two men, and that, I should say, is hardly a recommendation for Mr. Gibbon. Of course that alone is not enough to condemn him, but the intimacy is certainly a suspicious circumstance."

The two soon reached the house of Mr. Jennings, for the distance was only a quarter of a mile.

Mr. Jennings seemed a little surprised, but gave a kindly welcome to his unexpected guest. It occurred to him that he might have come to give some extra order for goods.

"You are surprised to see me," said Thorndike. "I came on a very important matter."

A look of inquiry came over the face of Mr. Jennings.

"There's a thief in the village - a guest at the hotel -

whom I recognize as one of the most expert burglars in the country."

"I think I know whom you mean, a man of moderate height, rather thick set, with small, black eyes and a slouch hat."

"Exactly."

"What can you tell me about him?"

Mr. Thorndike repeated the statement he had already made to Carl.

"Do you think our bank is in danger?" asked the manufacturer.

"Perhaps so, but the chief danger threatens you."

Mr. Jennings looked surprised.

"What makes you think so?"

"Because this man appears to be very intimate with your bookkeeper."

"How do you know that?" asked the little man, quickly.

"I refer you to Carl."

"Leonard Craig told me to-night that this man Stark spent every evening at his uncle's house."

Mr. Jennings looked troubled.

"I am sorry to hear this," he said. "I dislike to lose confidence in any man whom I have trusted."

"Have you noticed anything unusual in the demeanor of your bookkeeper of late?" asked Thorndike.

"Yes; he has appeared out of spirits and nervous."

"That would seem to indicate he is conspiring to rob you."

"This very day, noticing the change in him, I offered him a week's vacation. He promptly declined to take it."

"Of course. It would conflict with the plans of his confederate. I don't know the man, but I do know human nature, and I venture to predict that your safe will be opened within a week. Do you keep anything of value in it?"

"There are my books, which are of great value to me."

"But not to a thief. Anything else?"

"Yes; I have a tin box containing four thousand dollars in government bonds."

"Coupon or registered?"

"Coupon."

"Nothing could be better - for a burglar. What on earth could induce you to keep the bonds in your own safe?"

"To tell the truth, I considered them quite as safe there

as in the bank. Banks are more likely to be robbed than private individuals."

"Circumstances alter cases. Does anyone know that you have the bonds in your safe?"

"My bookkeeper is aware of it."

"Then, my friend, I caution you to remove the bonds from so unsafe a depository as soon as possible. Unless I am greatly mistaken, this man, Stark, has bought over your bookkeeper, and will have his aid in robbing you."

"What is your advice?"

"To remove the bonds this very evening," said Thorndike.

"Do you think the danger so pressing?"

"Of course I don't know that an attempt will be made to-night, but it is quite possible. Should it be so, you would have an opportunity to realize that delays are dangerous."

"Should Mr. Gibbon find, on opening the safe to-morrow morning, that the box is gone, it may lead to an attack upon my house."

"I wish you to leave the box in the safe."

"But I understand that you advised me to remove it."

"Not the box, but the bonds. Listen to my plan. Cut out some newspaper slips of about the same bulk as the bonds, put them in place of the bonds in the box, and quietly transfer the bonds in your pocket to your own house. To-morrow you can place them in the bank. Should no burglary be attempted, let the box remain in the safe, just as if its contents were valuable."

"Your advice is good, and I will adopt it," said Jennings, "and thank you for your valuable and friendly instruction."

"If agreeable to you I will accompany you to the office at once. The bonds cannot be removed too soon. Then if anyone sees us entering, it will be thought that you are showing me the factory. It will divert suspicion, even if we are seen by Stark or your bookkeeper."

"May I go, too?" asked Carl, eagerly.

"Certainly," said the manufacturer. "I know, Carl, that you are devoted to my interests. It is a comfort to know this, now that I have cause to suspect my bookkeeper."

It was only a little after nine. The night was moderately dark, and Carl was intrusted with a wax candle, which he put in his pocket for use in the office. They reached the factory without attracting attention, and entered by the office door.

Mr. Jennings opened the safe - he and the bookkeeper alone knew the combination - and with some anxiety took out the tin box. It was possible that the contents had already been removed. But no! on opening it, the bonds were found intact. According to Mr. Thorndike's advice, he transferred them to his pocket, and substituted folded paper. Then, replacing everything, the safe was once more locked, and the three left the office.

Mr. Thorndike returned to the hotel, and Mr. Jennings to his house, but Carl asked permission to remain out a while longer.

"It is on my mind that an attempt will be made to-night to rob the safe," he said. "I want to watch near the factory to see if my suspicion is correct."

"Very well, Carl, but don't stay out too long!" said his employer.

"Suppose I see them entering the office, sir?"

"Don't interrupt them! They will find themselves badly fooled. Notice only if Mr. Gibbon is of the party. I must know whether my bookkeeper is to be trusted."

CHAPTER XXIV.

THE BURGLARY.

Carl seated himself behind a stone wall on the opposite side of the street from the factory. The building was on the outskirts of the village, though not more than half a mile from the post office, and there was very little travel in that direction during the evening. This made it more favorable for thieves, though up to the present time no burglarious attempt had been made on it. Indeed, Milford had been exceptionally fortunate in that respect. Neighboring towns had been visited, some of them several times, but Milford had escaped.

The night was quite dark, but not what is called pitchy dark. As the eyes became accustomed to the obscurity, they were able to see a considerable distance. So it was with Carl. From his place of concealment he occasionally raised his head and looked across the way to the factory. An hour passed, and he grew tired. It didn't look as if the attempt were to be made that night. Eleven o'clock pealed out from the spire of the Baptist Church, a quarter of a mile away. Carl counted the strokes, and when the last died into silence, he said to himself:

"I will stay here about ten minutes longer. Then, if no one comes, I will give it up for tonight."

The time was nearly up when his quick ear caught a low murmur of voices. Instantly he was on the alert. Waiting till the sound came nearer, he ventured to raise his head for an instant above the top of the wall.

His heart beat with excitement when he saw two figures approaching. Though it was so dark, he recognized them by their size and outlines. They were Julius Gibbon, the bookkeeper, and Phil Stark, the stranger staying at the hotel.

Carl watched closely, raising his head for a few seconds at a time above the wall, ready to lower it should either glance in his direction. But neither of the men did so. Ignorant that they were suspected, it was the farthest possible from their thoughts that anyone would be on the watch.

Presently they came so near that Carl could hear their voices.

"I wish it was over," murmured Gibbon, nervously.

"Don't worry," said his companion. "There is no occasion for haste. Everybody in Milford is in bed and asleep, and we have several hours at our disposal."

"You must remember that my reputation is at stake. This night's work may undo me."

"My friend, you can afford to take the chances. Haven't I agreed to give you half the bonds?"

"I shall be suspected, and shall be obliged to stand my ground, while you will disappear from the scene."

"Two thousand dollars will pay you for some inconvenience. I don't see why you should be suspected.
You will be supposed to be fast asleep on your
virtuous couch, while some bad burglar is robbing your
worthy employer. Of course you will be thunderstruck
when in the morning the appalling discovery is made.
I'll tell you what will be a good dodge for you."

"Well?"

"Offer a reward of a hundred dollars from your own
purse for the discovery of the villain who has robbed
the safe and abstracted the bonds."

Phil Stark burst out into a loud guffaw as he uttered
these words.

"Hush!" said Gibbon, timidly. "I thought I heard some
one moving."

"What a timid fool you are!" muttered Stark, contemptuously. "If I had no more pluck, I'd hire myself out to
herd cows."

"It's a better business," said Gibbon, bitterly.

"Well, well, each to his taste! If you lose your place as
bookkeeper, you might offer your services to some
farmer. As for me, the danger, though there isn't much,
is just enough to make it exciting."

"I don't care for any such excitement," said Gibbon,
dispiritedly. "Why couldn't you have kept away and let
me earn an honest living?"

"Because I must live as well as you, my dear friend.

When this little affair is over, you will thank me for helping you to a good thing."

Of course all this conversation did not take place within Carl's hearing. While it was going on, the men had opened the office door and entered. Then, as Carl watched the window closely he saw a narrow gleam of light from a dark lantern illuminating the interior.

"Now they are at the safe," thought Carl.

We, who are privileged, will enter the office and watch the proceedings.

Gibbon had no difficulty in opening the safe, for he was acquainted with the combination. Stark thrust in his hand eagerly and drew out the box.

"This is what we want," he said, in a tone of satisfaction. "Have you a key that will open it?"

"No."

"Then I shall have to take box and all."

"Let us get through as soon as possible," said Gibbon, uneasily.

"You can close the safe, if you want to. There is nothing else worth taking?"

"No."

"Then we will evacuate the premises. Is there an old newspaper I can use to wrap up the box in? It might look suspicious if anyone should see it in our possession."

"Yes, here is one."

He handed a copy of a weekly paper to Phil Stark, who skillfully wrapped up the box, and placing it under his arm, went out of the office, leaving Gibbon to follow.

"Where will you carry it?" asked Gibbon.

"Somewhere out of sight where I can safely open it. I should have preferred to take the bonds, and leave the box in the safe. Then the bonds might not have been missed for a week or more."

"That would have been better."

That was the last that Carl heard. The two disappeared in the darkness, and Carl, raising himself from his place of concealment, stretched his cramped limbs and made the best of his way home. He thought no one would be up, but Mr. Jennings came out from the sitting-room, where he had flung himself on a lounge, and met Carl in the hall.

"Well?" he said.

"The safe has been robbed."

"Who did it?" asked the manufacturer, quickly.

"The two we suspected."

"Did you see Mr. Gibbon, then?"

"Yes; he was accompanied by Mr. Stark."

"You saw them enter the factory?"

"Yes, sir; I was crouching behind the stone wall on the other side of the road."

"How long were they inside?"

"Not over fifteen minutes - perhaps only ten."

"Mr. Gibbon knew the combination," said Jennings, quietly. "There was no occasion to lose time in breaking open the safe. There is some advantage in having a friend inside. Did you see them go out?"

"Yes, sir."

"Carrying the tin box with them?"

"Yes, sir. Mr. Stark wrapped it in a newspaper after they got outside."

"But you saw the tin box?"

"Yes."

"Then, if necessary, you can testify to it. I thought it possible that Mr. Gibbon might have a key to open it."

"I overheard Stark regretting that he could not open it so as to abstract the bonds and leave the box in the safe. In that case, he said, it might be some time before the robbery was discovered."

"He will himself make an unpleasant discovery when he opens the box. I don't think there is any call to pity him, do you, Carl?"

"No, sir. I should like to be within sight when he opens it."

The manufacturer laughed quietly.

"Yes," he said; "if I could see it I should feel repaid for the loss of the box. Let it be a lesson for you, my boy. Those who seek to enrich themselves by unlawful means are likely in the end to meet with disappointment."

"Do you think I need the lesson?" asked Carl, smiling.

"No, my lad. I am sure you don't. But you do need a good night's rest. Let us go to bed at once, and get what sleep we may. I won't allow the burglary to keep me awake."

He laughed in high good humor, and Carl went up to his comfortable room, where he soon lost all remembrance of the exciting scene of which he had been a witness.

Mr. Jennings went to the factory at the usual time the next morning.

As he entered the office the bookkeeper approached him pale and excited.

"Mr. Jennings," he said, hurriedly, "I have bad news for you."

"What is it, Mr. Gibbon?"

"When I opened the safe this morning, I discovered that the tin box had been stolen."

Mr. Jennings took the news quietly.

"Have you any suspicion who took it?" he asked.

"No, sir. I - I hope the loss is not a heavy one."

"I do not care to make the extent of the loss public. Were there any marks of violence? Was the safe broken open?"

"No, sir."

"Singular; is it not?"

"If you will allow me I will join in offering a reward for the discovery of the thief. I feel in a measure responsible."

"I will think of your offer, Mr. Gibbon."

"He suspects nothing," thought Gibbon, with a sigh of relief.

CHAPTER XXV.

STARK'S DISAPPOINTMENT.

Philip Stark went back to the hotel with the tin box under his arm. He would like to have entered the hotel without notice, but this was impossible, for the landlord's nephew was just closing up. Though not late for the city, it was very late for the country, and he looked surprised when Stark came in.

"I am out late," said Stark, with a smile.

"Yes."

"That is, late for Milford. In the city I never go to bed before midnight."

"Have you been out walking?"

"Yes."

"You found it rather dark, did you not?"

"It is dark as a pocket."

"You couldn't have found the walk a very pleasant one."

"You are right, my friend; but I didn't walk for pleasure. The fact is, I am rather worried about a business matter. I have learned that I am threatened with a heavy loss - an unwise investment in the West - and I wanted time to think it over and decide how to act."

"I see," answered the clerk, respectfully, for Stark's words led him to think that his guest was a man of wealth.

"I wish I was rich enough to be worried by such a cause," he said, jokingly.

"I wish you were. Some time I may be able to throw something in your way."

"Do you think it would pay me to go to the West?" asked the clerk, eagerly.

"I think it quite likely - if you know some one out in that section."

"But I don't know anyone."

"You know me," said Stark, significantly.

"Do you think you could help me to a place, Mr. Stark?"

"I think I could. A month from now write to me Col. Philip Stark, at Denver, Colorado, and I will see if I can find an opening for you."

"You are very kind, Mr. - I mean Col. Stark," said the clerk, gratefully.

"Oh, never mind about the title," returned Stark, smiling good-naturedly. "I only gave it to you just now, because everybody in Denver knows me as a colonel, and I am afraid a letter otherwise addressed would not reach me. By the way, I am sorry that I shall probably have to leave you to-morrow."

"So soon?"

"Yes; it's this tiresome business. I should not wonder if I might lose ten thousand dollars through the folly of my agent. I shall probably have to go out to right things."

"I couldn't afford to lose ten thousand dollars," said the young man, regarding the capitalist before him with deference.

"No, I expect not. At your age I wasn't worth ten thousand cents. Now - but that's neither here nor there. Give me a light, please, and I will go up to bed."

"He was about to say how much he is worth now," soliloquized the clerk. "I wish he had not stopped short. If I can't be rich myself, I like to talk with a rich man. There's hope for me, surely. He says that at my age he was not worth ten thousand cents. That is only a hundred dollars, and I am worth that. I must keep it to pay my expenses to Colorado, if he should send for me in a few weeks."

The young man had noticed with some curiosity the rather oddly-shaped bundle which Stark carried under his arm, but could not see his way clear to asking any questions about it. It seemed queer that Stark should have it with him while walking. Come to think of it, he remembered seeing him go out in the early evening, and he was quite confident that at that time he had no bundle with him. However, he was influenced only by a spirit of idle curiosity. He had no idea that the bundle was of any importance or value. The next day he changed his opinion on that subject.

Phil Stark went up to his chamber, and setting the lamp on the bureau, first carefully locked the door, and then removed the paper from the tin box. He eyed it lovingly, and tried one by one the keys he had in his pocket, but none exactly fitted.

As he was experimenting he thought with a smile of the night clerk from whom he had just parted.

"Stark," he soliloquized, addressing himself, "you are an old humbug. You have cleverly duped that unsophisticated young man downstairs. He looks upon you as a man of unbounded wealth, evidently, while, as a matter of fact, you are almost strapped. Let me see how much I have got left."

He took out his wallet, and counted out seven dollars and thirty-eight cents.

"That can hardly be said to constitute wealth," he reflected, "but it is all I have over and above the contents of this box. That makes all the difference. Gibbon is of opinion that there are four thousand dollars in bonds inside, and he expects me to give him half. Shall I do it? Not such a fool! I'll give him fifteen hundred and keep the balance myself.

That'll pay him handsomely, and the rest will be a good nestegg for me. If Gibbon is only half shrewd he will pull the wool over the eyes of that midget of an employer, and retain his place and comfortable salary. There will be no evidence against him, and he can pose as an innocent man. Bah! what a lot of humbug there is in the world. Well, well, Stark, you have your share, no doubt. Otherwise how would you make a living? To-morrow I must clear out from Milford, and give it a wide berth in future. I suppose there will be a great hue-and-cry about the robbery of the safe. It will be just as well for me to be somewhere else. I have already given the clerk a good reason for my sudden departure. Confound it, it's a great nuisance that I can't open this box! I would like to know before I go to bed just how much boodle I have acquired. Then I can decide how much to give Gibbon. If I dared I'd keep the whole, but he might make trouble."

Phil Stark, or Col. Philip Stark, as he had given his name, had a large supply of keys, but none of them seemed to fit the tin box.

"I am afraid I shall excite suspicion if I sit up any longer," thought Stark. "I will go to bed and get up early in the morning. Then I may succeed better in opening this plaguy box."

He removed his clothing and got into bed. The evening had been rather an exciting one, but the excitement was a pleasurable one, for he had succeeded in the plan which he and the bookkeeper had so ingeniously formed and carried out, and here within reach was the rich reward after which they had striven. Mr. Stark was not troubled with a conscience - that he had got rid of years ago - and he was filled with a comfortable consciousness of having retrieved his fortunes when they were on the wane. So, in a short time he fell asleep, and slept peacefully. Toward morning, however, he had a disquieting dream. It seemed to him that he awoke suddenly from slumber. and saw Gibbon leaving the room with the tin box under his arm. He awoke really with beads of perspiration upon his brow - awoke to see by the sun streaming in at his window that the morning was well advanced, and the tin box was still safe.

"Thank Heaven, it was but a dream!" he murmured. "I must get up and try once more to open the box."

The keys had all been tried, and had proved not to fit. Mr. Stark was equal to the emergency. He took from his pocket a button hook and bent it so as to make a pick, and after a little experimenting succeeded in turning the lock. He lifted the lid eagerly, and with distended eyes prepared to gloat upon the stolen bonds. But over his face there came a startling change. The ashy blue hue of disappointment succeeded the glowing, hopeful look. He snatched at one of the folded slips of paper and opened it. Alas! it was valueless, mere waste paper. He sank into a chair in a limp, hopeless posture, quite overwhelmed. Then he sprang up suddenly, and his expression changed to one of fury and menace.

"If Julius Gibbon has played this trick upon me," he said, between his set teeth, "he shall repent it - bitterly!"

Horatio Alger, Jr.

CHAPTER XXVI.

A DISAGREEABLE SURPRISE.

Philip Stark sat down to breakfast in a savage frame of mind. He wanted to be revenged upon Gibbon, whom he suspected of having deceived him by opening and appropriating the bonds, and then arranged to have him carry off the box filled with waste paper.

He sat at the table but five minutes, for he had little or no appetite.

From the breakfast room he went out on the piazza, and with corrugated brows smoked a cigar, but it failed to have the usual soothing effect.

If he had known the truth he would have left Milford without delay, but he was far from suspecting that the deception practiced upon him had been arranged by the man whom he wanted to rob. While there seemed little inducement for him to stay in Milford, he was determined to seek the bookkeeper, and ascertain whether, as he suspected, his confederate had in his possession the bonds which he had been scheming for. If so, he would compel him by threats to disgorge the larger portion, and then leave town at once.

But the problem was, how to see him. He felt that it

would be venturesome to go round to the factory, as by this time the loss might have been discovered. If only the box had been left, the discovery might be deferred.

Then a bright idea occurred to him. He must get the box out of his own possession, as its discovery would compromise him. Why could he not arrange to leave it somewhere on the premises of his confederate?

He resolved upon the instant to carry out the idea. He went up to his room, wrapped the tin box in a paper, and walked round to the house of the bookkeeper. The coast seemed to be clear, as he supposed it would be. He slipped into the yard, and swiftly entered an out-house. There was a large wooden chest, or box, which had once been used to store grain. Stark lifted the cover, dropped the box inside, and then, with a feeling of relief, walked out of the yard. But he had been observed. Mrs. Gibbon chanced to be looking out of a side window and saw him. She recognized him as the stranger who had been in the habit of spending recent evenings with her husband.

"What can he want here at this time?" she asked herself.

She deliberated whether she should go to the door and speak to Stark, but decided not to do so.

"He will call at the door if he has anything to say," she reflected.

Phil Stark walked on till he reached the factory. He felt that he must see Julius Gibbon, and satisfy himself as to the meaning of the mysterious substitution of waste paper for bonds.

When he reached a point where he could see into the office, he caught the eye of Leonard, who was sitting at the window. He beckoned for him to come out, and Leonard was glad to do so.

"Where are you going?" asked the bookkeeper, observing the boy's movement.

"Mr. Stark is just across the street, and he beckoned for me."

Julius Gibbon flushed painfully, and he trembled with nervous agitation, for he feared something had happened.

"Very well, go out, but don't stay long."

Leonard crossed the street and walked up to Stark, who awaited him, looking grim and stern.

"Your uncle is inside?" he asked.

"Yes, sir."

"Tell him I wish to see him at once - on business of importance."

"He's busy," said Leonard. "He doesn't leave the office in business hours."

"Tell him I must see him - do you hear? He'll come fast enough."

"I wonder what it's all about," thought Leonard, whose curiosity was naturally excited.

"Wait a minute!" said Stark, as he turned to go. "Is Jennings in?"

"No, sir, he has gone over to the next town."

"Probably the box has not been missed, then," thought Stark. "So much the better! I can find out how matters stand, and then leave town."

"Very well!" he said, aloud, "let your uncle understand that I must see him."

Leonard carried in the message. Gibbon made no objection, but took his hat and went out, leaving Leonard in charge of the office.

"Well, what is it?" he asked, hurriedly, as he reached Stark. "Is - is the box all right?"

"Look here, Gibbon," said Stark, harshly, "have you been playing any of your infernal tricks upon me?"

"I don't know what you mean," responded Gibbon, bewildered.

Stark eyed him sharply, but the bookkeeper was evidently sincere.

"Is there anything wrong?" continued the latter.

"Do you mean to tell me you didn't know that wretched box was filled with waste paper?"

"You don't mean it?" exclaimed Gibbon, in dismay.

"Yes, I do. I didn't open it till this morning, and in

Horatio Alger, Jr.

place of government bonds, I found only folded slips of newspaper."

By this time Gibbon was suspicious. Having no confidence in Stark, it occurred to him that it was a ruse to deprive him of his share of the bonds.

"I don't believe you," he said. "You want to keep all the bonds for yourself, and cheat me out of my share."

"I wish to Heaven you were right. If there had been any bonds, I would have acted on the square. But somebody had removed them, and substituted paper. I suspected you."

"I am ready to swear that this has happened without my knowledge," said Gibbon, earnestly.

"How, then, could it have occurred?" asked Stark.

"I don't know, upon my honor. Where is the box?"

"I - have disposed of it."

"You should have waited and opened it before me."

"I asked you if you had a key that would open it. I wanted to open it last evening in the office."

"True."

"You will see after a while that I was acting on the square. You can open it for yourself at your leisure."

"How can I? I don't know where it is."

"Then I can enlighten you," said Stark, maliciously. "When you go home, you will find it in a chest in your woodshed."

Gibbon turned pale.

"You don't mean to say you have carried it to my house?" he exclaimed, in dismay.

"Yes, I do. I had no further use for it, and thought you had the best claim to it."

"But, good heavens! if it is found there I shall be suspected."

"Very probably," answered Stark, coolly. "Take my advice and put it out of the way."

"How could you be so inconsiderate?"

"Because I suspected you of playing me a trick."

"I swear to you, I didn't."

"Then somebody has tricked both of us. Has Mr. Jennings discovered the disappearance of the box?"

"Yes, I told him."

"When?"

"When he came to the office."

"What did he say?"

"He took the matter coolly. He didn't say much."

"Where is he?"

"Gone to Winchester on business."

"Look here! Do you think he suspects you?"

"I am quite sure not. That is why I told him about the robbery."

"He might suspect me."

"He said nothing about suspecting anybody."

"Do you think he removed the bonds and substituted paper?"

"I don't think so."

"If this were the case we should both be in a serious plight. I think I had better get out of town. You will have to lend me ten dollars."

"I don't see how I can, Stark."

"You must!" said Stark, sternly, "or I will reveal the whole thing. Remember, the box is on your premises."

"Heavens! what a quandary I am in," said the book-keeper, miserably. "That must be attended to at once. Why couldn't you put it anywhere else?"

"I told you that I wanted to be revenged upon you."

"I wish you had never come to Milford," groaned the bookkeeper.

"I wish I hadn't myself, as things have turned out."

They prepared to start for Gibbon's house, when Mr. Jennings drove up. With him were two tall muscular men, whom Stark and Gibbon eyed uneasily. The two strangers jumped out of the carriage and advanced toward the two confederates.

"Arrest those men!" said Jennings, in a quiet tone. "I charge them with opening and robbing my safe last night about eleven o'clock."

CHAPTER XXVII.

BROUGHT TO BAY.

Phil Stark made an effort to get away, but the officer was too quick for him. In a trice he was handcuffed.

"What is the meaning of this outrage?" demanded Stark, boldly.

"I have already explained," said the manufacturer, quietly.

"You are quite on the wrong tack," continued Stark, brazenly. "Mr. Gibbon was just informing me that the safe had been opened and robbed. It is the first I knew of it."

Julius Gibbon seemed quite prostrated by his arrest. He felt it necessary to say something, and followed the lead of his companion.

"You will bear me witness, Mr. Jennings," he said, "that I was the first to inform you of the robbery. If I had really committed the burglary, I should have taken care to escape during the night."

"I should be glad to believe in your innocence," rejoined the manufacturer. "but I know more about this matter than you suppose."

"I won't answer for Mr. Gibbon," said Stark, who cared nothing for his confederate, if he could contrive to effect his own escape. "Of course he had opportunities, as bookkeeper, which an outsider could not have."

Gibbon eyed his companion in crime distrustfully. He saw that Stark was intending to throw him over.

"I am entirely willing to have my room at the hotel searched," continued Stark, gathering confidence. "If you find any traces of the stolen property there, you are welcome to make the most of them. I have no doubt Mr. Gibbon will make you the same offer in regard to his house."

Gibbon saw at once the trap which had been so craftily prepared for him. He knew that any search of his premises would result in the discovery of the tin box, and had no doubt that Stark would he ready to testify to any falsehood likely to fasten the guilt upon him. His anger was roused and he forgot his prudence.

"You - scoundrel!" he hissed between his closed teeth.

"You seem excited," sneered Stark. "Is it possible that you object to the search?"

"If the missing box is found on my premises," said Gibbon, in a white heat, "it is because you have concealed it there."

Phil Stark shrugged his shoulders.

"I think, gentlemen," he said, "that settles it. I am

afraid Mr Gibbon is guilty. I shall be glad to assist you to recover the stolen property. Did the box contain much that was of value?"

"I must caution you both against saying anything that will compromise you," said one of the officers.

"I have nothing to conceal," went on Stark, brazenly. "I am obliged to believe that this man committed the burglary. It is against me that I have been his companion for the last week or two, but I used to know him, and that will account for it."

The unhappy bookkeeper saw the coils closing around him.

"I hope you will see your way to release me," said Stark, addressing himself to Mr. Jennings. "I have just received information that my poor mother is lying dangerously sick in Cleveland, and I am anxious to start for her bedside to-day."

"Why did you come round here this morning?" asked Mr. Jennings.

"To ask Mr. Gibbon to repay me ten dollars which he borrowed of me the other day," returned Stark, glibly.

"You - liar!" exclaimed Gibbon, angrily.

"I am prepared for this man's abuse," said Stark. "I don't mind admitting now that a few days since he invited me to join him in the robbery of the safe. I threatened to inform you of his plan, and he promised to give it up. I supposed he had done so, but it is clear to me now that he carried out his infamous scheme."

Mr. Jennings looked amused. He admired Stark's brazen effrontery.

"What have you to say to this charge, Mr. Gibbon?" he asked.

"Only this, sir, that I was concerned in the burglary."

"He admits it!" said Stark, triumphantly.

"But this man forced me to it. He threatened to write you some particulars of my past history which would probably have lost me my position if I did not agree to join him in the conspiracy. I was weak, and yielded. Now he is ready to betray me to save himself."

"Mr. Jennings," said Stark, coldly, "you will know what importance to attach to the story of a self-confessed burglar. Gibbon, I hope you will see the error of your ways, and restore to your worthy employer the box of valuable property which you stole from his safe."

"This is insufferable!" cried the bookkeeper "You are a double-dyed traitor, Phil Stark. You were not only my accomplice, but you instigated the crime."

"You will find it hard to prove this," sneered Stark. "Mr. Jennings, I demand my liberty. If you have any humanity you will not keep me from the bedside of my dying mother." "I admire your audacity, Mr. Stark," observed the manufacturer, quietly. "Don't suppose for a moment that I give the least credit to your statements."

"Thank you, sir," said Gibbon. "I'm ready to accept the

consequences of my act, but I don't want that scoundrel and traitor to go free."

"You can't prove anything against me," said Stark, doggedly, "unless you accept the word of a self-confessed burglar, who is angry with me because I would not join him."

"All these protestations it would be better for you to keep till your trial begins, Mr. Stark," said the manufacturer. "However, I think it only fair to tell you that I am better informed about you and your conspiracy than you imagine. Will you tell me where you were at eleven o'clock last evening?"

"I was in my room at the hotel - no, I was taking a walk. I had received news of my mother's illness, and I was so much disturbed and grieved that I could not remain indoors."

"You were seen to enter the office of this factory with Mr. Gibbon, and after ten minutes came out with the tin box under your arm."

"Who saw me?" demanded Stark, uneasily.

Carl Crawford came forward and answered this question.

"I did!" he said.

"A likely story! You were in bed and asleep."

"You are mistaken. I was on watch behind the stone wall just opposite. If you want proof, I can repeat some of the conversation that passed between you and

Mr. Gibbon."

Without waiting for the request, Carl rehearsed some of the talk already recorded in a previous chapter.

Phil Stark began to see that things were getting serious for him, but he was game to the last.

"I deny it," he said, in a loud voice.

"Do you also deny it, Mr. Gibbon?" asked Mr. Jennings.

"No, sir; I admit it," replied Gibbon, with a triumphant glance at his foiled confederate.

"This is a conspiracy against an innocent man," said Stark, scowling. "You want to screen your bookkeeper, if possible. No one has ever before charged me with crime."

"Then how does it happen, Mr. Stark, that you were confined at the Joliet penitentiary for a term of years?"

"Did he tell you this?" snarled Stark, pointing to Gibbon.

"No."

"Who then?"

"A customer of mine from Chicago. He saw you at the hotel, and informed Carl last evening of your character. Carl, of course, brought the news to me. It was in consequence of this information that I myself removed the bonds from the box, early in the evening, and substituted strips of paper. Your enterprise, therefore, would have availed you little even if you had succeeded in getting off scot-free."

"I see the game is up," said Stark, throwing off the mask. "It's true that I have been in the Joliet penitentiary. It was there that I became acquainted with your bookkeeper," he added, maliciously. "Let him deny it if he dare."

"I shall not deny it. It is true," said Gibbon. "But I had resolved to live an honest life in future, and would have done so if this man had not pressed me into crime by his threats."

"I believe you, Mr. Gibbon," said the manufacturer, gently, "and I will see that this is counted in your favor. And now, gentlemen, I think there is no occasion for further delay."

The two men were carried to the lockup and in due time were tried. Stark was sentenced to ten years' imprisonment, Gibbon to five. At the end of two years, at the intercession of Mr. Jennings, he was pardoned, and furnished with money enough to go to Australia, where, his past character unknown, he was able to make an honest living, and gain a creditable position.

CHAPTER XXVIII.

AFTER A YEAR.

Twelve months passed without any special incident. With Carl it was a period of steady and intelligent labor and progress. He had excellent mechanical talent, and made remarkable advancement. He was not content with attention to his own work, but was a careful observer of the work of others, so that in one year he learned as much of the business as most boys would have done in three.

When the year was up, Mr. Jennings detained him after supper.

"Do you remember what anniversary this is, Carl?" he asked, pleasantly.

"Yes, sir; it is the anniversary of my going into the factory."

"Exactly. How are you satisfied with the year and its work?"

"I have been contented and happy, Mr. Jennings; and I feel that I owe my happiness and content to you."

Mr. Jennings looked pleased.

Horatio Alger, Jr.

"I am glad you say so," he said, "but it is only fair to add that your own industry and intelligence have much to do with the satisfactory results of the year."

"Thank you, sir."

"The superintendent tells me that outside of your own work you have a general knowledge of the business which would make you a valuable assistant to himself in case he needed one."

Carl's face glowed with pleasure.

"I believe in being thorough," he said, "and I am interested in every department of the business."

"Before you went into the factory you had not done any work."

"No, sir; I had attended school."

"It was not a bad preparation for business, but in some cases it gives a boy disinclination for manual labor."

"Yes; I wouldn't care to work with my hands all my life."

"I don't blame you for that. You have qualified yourself for something better. How much do I pay you?"

"I began on two dollars a week and my board. At the end of six months you kindly advanced me to four dollars."

"I dare say you have found it none too much for

your wants."

Carl smiled.

"I have saved forty dollars out of it," he answered.

Mr. Jennings looked pleased.

"You have done admirably," he said, warmly. "Forty dollars is not a large sum, but in laying it by you have formed a habit that will be of great service to you in after years. I propose to raise you to ten dollars a week."

"But, sir, shall I earn so much? You are very kind, but I am afraid you will be a loser by your liberality."

Mr. Jennings smiled.

"You are partly right," he said. "Your services at present are hardly worth the sum I have agreed to pay, that is, in the factory, but I shall probably impose upon you other duties of an important nature soon."

"If you do, sir, I will endeavor to meet your expectations."

"How would you like to take a journey Carl?"

"Very much, sir."

"I think of sending you - to Chicago."

Carl, who had thought perhaps of a fifty-mile trip, looked amazed, but his delight was equal to his surprise. He had always wished to see the West, though Chicago can hardly be called a Western city now, since between it and the Pacific there is a broad belt of land two thousand miles in extent.

"Do you think I am competent?" he asked, modestly.

"I cannot say positively, but I think so," answered Mr. Jennings.

"Then I shall be delighted to go. Will it be very soon?"

"Yes, very soon. I shall want you to start next Monday."

"I will be ready, sir."

"And I may as well explain what are to be your duties. I am, as you know, manufacturing a special line of chairs which I am desirous of introducing to the trade. I shall give you the names of men in my line in Albany, Buffalo, Cleveland and Chicago, and it will be your duty to call upon them, explain the merits of the chair, and solicit orders. In other words, you will be a traveling salesman or drummer. I shall pay your traveling expenses, ten dollars a week, and, if your orders exceed a certain limit, I shall give you a commission on the surplus."

"Suppose I don't reach that limit?"

"I shall at all events feel that you have done your best. I will instruct you a little in your duties between now and the time of your departure. I should myself like to go in your stead, but I am needed here. There are, of course, others in my employ, older than yourself, whom I might send, but I have an idea that you will prove to be a good salesman."

"I will try to be, sir."

On Monday morning Carl left Milford, reached New York in two hours and a half and, in accordance with the directions of Mr. Jennings, engaged passage and a stateroom on one of the palatial night lines of Hudson River steamers to Albany. The boat was well filled with passengers, and a few persons were unable to procure staterooms.

Carl, however, applied in time, and obtained an excellent room. He deposited his gripsack therein, and then took a seat on deck, meaning to enjoy as long as possible the delightful scenery for which the Hudson is celebrated. It was his first long journey, and for this reason Carl enjoyed it all the more. He could not but contrast his present position and prospects with those of a year ago, when, helpless and penniless, he left an unhappy home to make his own way.

"What a delightful evening!" said a voice at his side.

Turning, Carl saw sitting by him a young man of about thirty, dressed in somewhat pretentious style and wearing eyeglasses. He was tall and thin, and had sandy side whiskers.

"Yes, it is a beautiful evening," replied Carl, politely.

"And the scenery is quite charming. Have you ever been all the way up the river?"

"No, but I hope some day to take a day trip."

"Just so. I am not sure but I prefer the Rhine, with its romantic castles and vineclad hills."

"Have you visited Europe, then?" asked Carl.

"Oh, yes, several times. I have a passion for traveling. Our family is wealthy, and I have been able to go where I pleased."

"That must be very pleasant."

"It is. My name is Stuyvesant - one of the old Dutch families."

Carl was not so much impressed, perhaps, as he should have been by this announcement, for he knew very little of fashionable life in New York.

"You don't look like a Dutchman," he said, smiling.

"I suppose you expected a figure like a beer keg," rejoined Stuyvesant, laughing. "Some of my fore-fathers may have answered that description, but I am not built that way. Are you traveling far?"

"I may go as far as Chicago."

"Is anyone with you?"

"No."

"Perhaps you have friends in Chicago?"

"Not that I am aware of. I am traveling on business."

"Indeed; you are rather young for a business man."

"I am sixteen."

"Well, that cannot exactly be called venerable."

"No, I suppose not."

"By the way, did you succeed in getting a stateroom?"

"Yes, I have a very good one."

"You're in luck, on my word. I was just too late. The man ahead of me took the last room."

"You can get a berth, I suppose."

"But that is so common. Really, I should not know how to travel without a stateroom. Have you anyone with you?"

"No."

"If you will take me in I will pay the entire expense."

Carl hesitated. He preferred to be alone, but he was of an obliging disposition, and he knew that there were two berths in the stateroom.

"If it will be an accommodation," he said, "I will let you occupy the room with me, Mr. Stuyvesant."

"Will you, indeed! I shall esteem it a very great favor. Where is your room?"

"I will show you."

Carl led the way to No. 17, followed by his new

Horatio Alger, Jr.

acquaintance. Mr. Stuyvesant seemed very much pleased, and insisted on paying for the room at once. Carl accepted half the regular charges, and so the bargain was made.

At ten o'clock the two travelers retired to bed. Carl was tired and went to sleep at once. He slept through the night. When he awoke in the morning the boat was in dock. He heard voices in the cabin, and the noise of the transfer of baggage and freight to the wharf.

"I have overslept myself," he said, and jumped up, hurriedly. He looked into the upper berth, but his roommate was gone. Something else was gone, too - his valise, and a wallet which he had carried in the pocket of his trousers.

CHAPTER XXIX.

THE LOST BANK BOOK.

Carl was not long in concluding that he had been robbed by his roommate. It was hard to believe that a Stuyvesant - a representative of one of the old Dutch families of New Amsterdam - should have stooped to such a discreditable act. Carl was sharp enough, however, to doubt the genuineness of Mr. Stuyvesant's claims to aristocratic lineage. Meanwhile he blamed himself for being so easily duped by an artful adventurer.

To be sure, it was not as bad as it might be. His pocketbook only contained ten dollars in small bills. The balance of his money he had deposited for safe keeping in the inside pocket of his vest. This he had placed under his pillow, and so it had escaped the notice of the thief.

The satchel contained a supply of shirts, underclothing, etc., and he was sorry to lose it. The articles were not expensive, but it would cost him from a dozen to fifteen dollars to replace them.

Carl stepped to the door of his stateroom and called a servant who was standing near.

"How long have we been at the pier?" he asked.

"About twenty minutes, sir."

"Did you see my roommate go out?"

"A tall young man in a light overcoat?"

"Yes."

"Yes, sir. I saw him."

"Did you notice whether he carried a valise in his hand?"

"A gripsack? Yes, sir."

"A small one?"

"Yes, sir."

"It was mine."

"You don't say so, sir! And such a respectable-lookin' gemman, sir."

"He may have looked respectable, but he was a thief all the same."

"You don't say? Did he take anything else, sir?"

"He took my pocketbook."

"Well, well! He was a rascal, sure! But maybe it dropped on the floor."

Carl turned his attention to the carpet, but saw nothing of the lost pocketbook. He did find, however, a small book in a brown cover, which Stuyvesant had probably dropped. Picking it up, he discovered that it was a bank book on the Sixpenny Savings Bank of Albany, standing in the name of Rachel Norris, and numbered 17,310.

"This is stolen property, too," thought Carl. "I wonder if there is much in it."

Opening the book he saw that there were three entries, as follows:

    1883. Jan. 23. Five hundred dollars.
    "   June 10. Two hundred dollars.
    "   Oct. 21. One hundred dollars.

There was besides this interest credited to the amount of seventy-five dollars. The deposits, therefore, made a grand total of $875.

No doubt Mr. Stuyvesant had stolen this book, but had not as yet found an opportunity of utilizing it.

"What's dat?" asked the colored servant.

"A savings bank book. My roommate must have dropped it. It appears to belong to a lady named Rachel Norris. I wish I could get it to her."

"Is she an Albany lady, sir?"

"I don't know."

"You might look in the directory."

"So I will. It is a good idea."

"I hope the gemman didn't take all your money, sir."

"No; he didn't even take half of it. I only wish I had been awake when the boat got to the dock."

"I would have called you, sir, if you had asked me."

"I am not much used to traveling. I shall know better next time what to do."

The finding of the bank book partially consoled Carl for the loss of his pocketbook and gripsack. He was glad to be able to defeat Stuyvesant in one of his nefarious schemes, and to be the instrument of returning Miss Norris her savings bank book.

When he left the boat he walked along till he reached a modest-looking hotel, where he thought the charges would be reasonable. He entered, and, going to the desk, asked if he could have a room.

"Large or small?" inquired the clerk.

"Small."

"No. 67. Will you go up now?"

"Yes, sir."

"Any baggage?"

"No; I had it stolen on the boat."

The clerk looked a little suspicious.

"We must require pay in advance, then," he said.

"Certainly," answered Carl, pulling out a roll of bills. I suppose you make special terms to commercial travelers?"

"Are you a drummer?"

"Yes. I represent Henry Jennings, of Milford, New York."

"All right, sir. Our usual rates are two dollars a day. To you they will be a dollar and a quarter."

"Very well; I will pay you for two days. Is breakfast ready?"

"It is on the table, sir."

"Then I will go in at once. I will go to my room afterwards."

In spite of his loss, Carl had a hearty appetite, and did justice to the comfortable breakfast provided. He bought a morning paper, and ran his eye over the advertising columns. He had never before read an Albany paper, and wished to get an idea of the city in its business aspect. It occurred to him that there might be an advertisement of the lost bank book. But no such notice met his eyes.

He went up to his room, which was small and plainly furnished, but looked comfortable. Going down again to the office, he looked into the Albany directory to see if he could find the name of Rachel Norris.

There was a Rebecca Norris, who was put down as a dressmaker, but that was as near as he came to Rachel Norris.

Then he set himself to looking over the other members of the Norris family. Finally he picked out Norris & Wade, furnishing goods, and decided to call at the store and inquire if they knew any lady named Rachel Norris. The prospect of gaining information in this way did not seem very promising, but no other course presented itself, and Carl determined to follow up the clew, slight as it was.

Though unacquainted with Albany streets, he had little difficulty in finding the store of Norris & Wade. It was an establishment of good size, well supplied with attractive goods. A clerk came forward to wait upon Carl.

"What can I show you?" he asked.

"You may show me Mr. Norris, if you please," responded Carl, with a smile.

"He is in the office," said the clerk, with an answering smile.

Carl entered the office and saw Mr. Norris, a man of middle age, partially bald, with a genial, business-like manner.

"Well, young man?" he said, looking at Carl inquiringly.

"You must excuse me for troubling you, sir," said Carl, who was afraid Mr. Norris would laugh at him, "but I thought you might direct me to Rachel Norris."

Mr. Norris looked surprised.

"What do you want of Rachel Norris?" he asked, abruptly.

"I have a little business with her," answered Carl.

"Of what nature?"

"Excuse me, but I don't care to mention it at present."

"Humph! you are very cautious for a young man, or rather boy."

"Isn't that a good trait, sir?"

"Good, but unusual. Are you a schoolboy?"

"No, sir; I am a drummer."

Mr. Norris put on a pair of glasses and scrutinized Carl more closely.

"I should like to see - just out of curiosity - the man that you travel for," he said.

"I will ask him to call whenever he visits Albany. There is his card."

Mr. Norris took it.

"Why, bless my soul!" he exclaimed. "It is Henry Jennings, an old schoolmate of mine."

"And a good business man, even if he has sent out such a young drummer."

"I should say so. There must be something in you, or he wouldn't have trusted you. How is Jennings?"

"He is well, sir - well and prosperous."

"That is good news. Are you in his employ?"

"Yes, sir. This is the first time I have traveled for him."

"How far are you going?"

"As far as Chicago."

"I don't see what you can have to do with Rachel Norris. However, I don't mind telling you that she is my aunt, and - well, upon my soul! Here she is now."

And he ran hastily to greet a tall, thin lady, wearing a black shawl, who at that moment entered the office.

CHAPTER XXX.

AN ECCENTRIC WOMAN.

Miss Norris dropped into a chair as if she were fatigued.

"Well, Aunt Rachel, how are you feeling this morning?" asked her nephew.

"Out of sorts," was the laconic reply.

"I am very sorry for that. I suppose there is reason for it."

"Yes; I've been robbed."

"Indeed!" said Mr. Norris. "Lost your purse? I wonder more ladies are not robbed, carrying their money as carelessly as they do."

"That isn't it. I am always careful, as careful as any man."

"Still you got robbed."

"Yes, but of a bank book."

Here Carl became attentive. It was clear that he would

Horatio Alger, Jr.

not have to look any farther for the owner of the book he had found in his stateroom.

"What kind of a bank book?" inquired Mr. Norris.

"I had nearly a thousand dollars deposited in the Sixpenny Savings Bank. I called at the bank to make some inquiries about interest, and when I came out I presume some rascal followed me and stole the book -"

"Have you any idea who took it?"

"I got into the horse cars, near the bank; next to me sat a young man in a light overcoat. There was no one on the other side of me. I think he must have taken it."

"That was Stuyvesant," said Carl to himself.

"When did this happen, Aunt Rachel?"

"Three days since."

"Why didn't you do something about it before?"

"I did. I advertised a reward of twenty-five dollars to anyone who would restore it to me."

"There was no occasion for that. By giving notice at the bank, they would give you a new book after a time."

"I preferred to recover the old one. Besides, I thought I would like to know what became of it."

"I can tell you, Miss Norris," said Carl, who thought it time to speak.

Hitherto Miss Norris had not seemed aware of Carl's presence. She turned abruptly and surveyed him through her glasses.

"Who are you?" she asked.

This might seem rude, but it was only Miss Rachel's way.

"My name is Carl Crawford."

"Do I know you?"

"No, Miss Norris, but I hope you will."

"Humph! that depends. You say you know what became of my bank book?"

"Yes, Miss Norris."

"Well?"

"It was taken by the young man who sat next to you."

"How do you know?"

"He robbed me last night on the way from New York in a Hudson River steamboat."

"That doesn't prove that he robbed me. I was robbed here in this city."

"What do you say to this?" asked Carl, displaying the bank book.

"Bless me! That is my book. Where did you get it?"

Carl told his story briefly, how, on discovering that he had been robbed, he explored the stateroom and found the bank book.

"Well, well, I am astonished! And how did you know Mr. Norris was my nephew?"

"I didn't know. I didn't know anything about him or you, but finding his name in the directory, I came here to ask if he knew any such person."

"You are a smart boy, and a good, honest one," said Miss Norris. "You have earned the reward, and shall have it."

"I don't want any reward, Miss Norris," rejoined Carl. "I have had very little trouble in finding you."

"That is of no consequence. I offered the reward, and Rachel Norris is a woman of her word."

She thrust her hand into her pocket, and drew out a wallet, more suitable to a man's use. Openings this, she took out three bills, two tens and a five, and extended them toward Carl.

"I don't think I ought to take this money, Miss Norris," said Carl, reluctantly.

"Did that rascal rob you, too?"

"Yes."

"Of how much?"

"Ten dollars in money and some underclothing."

"Very well! This money will go toward making up your loss. You are not rich, I take it?"

"Not yet."

"I am, and can afford to give you this money. There, take it."

"Thank you, Miss Norris."

"I want to ask one favor of you. If you ever come across that young man in the light overcoat, have him arrested, and let me know."

"I will, Miss Norris."

"Do you live in Albany?"

Carl explained that he was traveling on business, and should leave the next day if he could get through.

"How far are you going?"

"To Chicago."

"Can you attend to some business for me there?"

"Yes, if it won't take too long a time."

"Good! Come round to my house to supper at six o'clock, and I will tell you about it. Henry, write my address on a piece of paper, and give it to this young man."

Henry Norris smiled, and did as his aunt requested.

"You have considerable confidence in this young man?" he said.

"I have."

"You may be mistaken."

"Rachel Norris is not often mistaken."

"I will accept your invitation with pleasure, Miss Norris," said Carl, bowing politely. "Now, as I have some business to attend to, I will bid you both good-morning."

As Carl went out, Miss Norris said: "Henry, that is a remarkable boy."

"I think favorably of him myself. He is in the employ of an old schoolmate of mine, Henry Jennings, of Milford. By the way, what business are you going to put into his hands?"

"A young man who has a shoe store on State Street has asked me for a loan of two thousand dollars to extend his business. His name is John French, and his mother was an old schoolmate of mine, though some years younger. Now I know nothing of him. If he is a sober, steady, industrious young man, I may comply with his request. This boy will investigate and report to me."

"And you will be guided by his report?"

"Probably."

"Aunt Rachel, you are certainly very eccentric."

"I may be, but I am not often deceived."

"Well, I hope you won't be this time. The boy seems to me a very good boy, but you can't put an old head on young shoulders."

"Some boys have more sense than men twice their age."

"You don't mean me, I hope, Aunt Rachel," said Mr. Norris, smiling.

"Indeed, I don't. I shall not flatter you by speaking of you as only twice this boy's age."

"I see, Aunt Rachel, there is no getting the better of you."

Meanwhile Carl was making business calls. He obtained a map of the city, and located the different firms on which he proposed to call. He had been furnished with a list by Mr. Jennings. He was everywhere pleasantly received - in some places with an expression of surprise at his youth - but when he began to talk he proved to be so well informed upon the subject of his call that any prejudice excited by his age quickly vanished. He had the satisfaction of securing several unexpectedly large orders for the chair, and transmitting them to Mr. Jennings by the afternoon mail.

He got through his business at four o'clock, and rested for an hour or more at his hotel. Then he arranged his toilet, and set out for the residence of Miss Rachel Norris.

It was rather a prim-looking, three-story house, such as might be supposed to belong to a maiden lady. He was ushered into a sitting-room on the second floor, where Miss Norris soon joined him.

"I am glad to see you, my young friend," she said, cordially. "You are in time."

"I always try to be, Miss Norris."

"It is a good way to begin."

Here a bell rang.

"Supper is ready," she said. "Follow me downstairs."

Carl followed the old lady to the rear room on the lower floor. A small table was set in the center of the apartment.

"Take a seat opposite me," said Miss Norris.

There were two other chairs, one on each side - Carl wondered for whom they were set. No sooner were he and Miss Norris seated than two large cats approached the table, and jumped up, one into each chair. Carl looked to see them ordered away, but instead, Miss Norris nodded pleasantly, saying: "That's right, Jane and Molly, you are punctual at meals."

The two cats eyed their mistress gravely, and began to purr contentedly.

CHAPTER XXXI.

CARL TAKES SUPPER WITH MISS NORRIS.

"This is my family," said Miss Norris, pointing to the cats.

"I like cats," said Carl.

"Do you?" returned Miss Norris, looking pleased. "Most boys tease them. Do you see poor Molly's ear? That wound came from a stone thrown by a bad boy."

"Many boys are cruel," said Carl, "but I remember that my mother was very fond of cats, and I have always protected them from abuse."

As he spoke he stroked Molly, who purred an acknowledgment of his attention. This completed the conquest of Miss Norris, who inwardly decided that Carl was the finest boy she had ever met. After she had served Carl from the dishes on the table, she poured out two saucers of milk and set one before each cat, who, rising upon her hind legs, placed her forepaws on the table, and gravely partook of the refreshments provided. Jane and Molly were afterwards regaled with cold meat, and then, stretching themselves out on their chairs, closed their eyes in placid content.

Horatio Alger, Jr.

During the meal Miss Norris questioned Carl closely as to his home experiences. Having no reason for concealment Carl frankly related his troubles with his stepmother, eliciting expressions of sympathy and approval from his hostess.

"Your stepmother must be an ugly creature?" she said.

"I am afraid I am prejudiced against her," said Carl, "but that is my opinion."

"Your father must be very weak to be influenced against his own son by such a woman."

Carl winced a little at this outspoken criticism, for he was attached to his father in spite of his unjust treatment.

"My father is an invalid," he said, apologetically, "and I think he yielded for the sake of peace."

"All the same, he ought not to do it," said Miss Norris. "Do you ever expect to live at home again?"

"Not while my stepmother is there," answered Carl. "But I don't know that I should care to do so under any circumstances, as I am now receiving a business training. I should like to make a little visit home," he added, thoughtfully, "and perhaps I may do so after I return from Chicago. I shall have no favors to ask, and shall feel independent."

"If you ever need a home," said Miss Norris, abruptly, "come here. You will be welcome."

"Thank you very much," said Carl, gratefully. "It is all

the more kind in you since you have known me so short a time."

"I have known you long enough to judge of you," said the maiden lady. "And now if you won't have anything more we will go into the next room and talk business."

Carl followed her into the adjoining room, and Miss Norris at once plunged into the subject. She handed him a business card bearing this inscription:

JOHN FRENCH,
BOOTS, SHOES AND RUBBER GOODS,
42a State Street, CHICAGO.

"This young man wants me to lend him two thousand dollars to extend his business," she said. "He is the son of an old school friend, and I am willing to oblige him if he is a sober, steady and economical business man. I want you to find out whether this is the case and report to me."

"Won't that be difficult?" asked Carl.

"Are you afraid to undertake anything that is difficult?"

"No," answered Carl, with a smile. "I was only afraid I might not do the work satisfactorily."

"I shall give you no instructions," said Miss Norris. "I shall trust to your good judgment. I will give you a letter to Mr. French, which you can use or not, as you think wise. Of course, I shall see that you are paid for your trouble."

"Thank you," said Carl. "I hope my services may be

worth compensation."

"I don't know how you are situated as to money, but I can give you some in advance," and the old lady opened her pocketbook.

"No, thank you, Miss Norris; I shall not need it. I might have been short if you had not kindly paid me a reward for a slight service."

"Slight, indeed! If you had lost a bank book like mine you would be glad to get it back at such a price. If you will catch the rascal who stole it I will gladly pay you as much more."

"I wish I might for my own sake, but I am afraid it would be too late to recover my money and clothing."

At an early hour Carl left the house, promising to write to Miss Norris from Chicago.

CHAPTER XXXII.

A STARTLING DISCOVERY.

"Well," thought Carl, as he left the house where he had been so hospitably entertained, "I shall not lack for business. Miss Norris seems to have a great deal of confidence in me, considering that I am a stranger. I will take care that she does not repent it."

"Can you give a poor man enough money to buy a cheap meal?" asked a plaintive voice.

Carl scanned the applicant for charity closely. He was a man of medium size, with a pair of small eyes, and a turnup nose. His dress was extremely shabby, and he had the appearance of one who was on bad terms with fortune. There was nothing striking about his appearance, yet Carl regarded him with surprise and wonder. Despite the difference in age, he bore a remarkable resemblance to his stepbrother, Peter Cook.

"I haven't eaten anything for twenty-four hours," continued the tramp, as he may properly be called. "It's a hard world to such as me, boy."

"I should judge so from your looks," answered Carl.

"Indeed you are right. I was born to ill luck."

Carl had some doubts about this. Those who represent themselves as born to ill luck can usually trace the ill luck to errors or shortcomings of their own. There are doubtless inequalities of fortune, but not as great as many like to represent. Of two boys who start alike one may succeed, and the other fail, but in nine cases out of ten the success or failure may be traced to a difference in the qualities of the boys.

"Here is a quarter if that will do you any good," said Carl.

The man clutched at it with avidity.

"Thank you. This will buy me a cup of coffee and a plate of meat, and will put new life into me."

He was about to hurry away, but Carl felt like questioning him further. The extraordinary resemblance between this man and his stepbrother led him to think it possible that there might be a relationship between them. Of his stepmother's family he knew little or nothing. His father had married her on short acquaintance, and she was very reticent about her former life. His father was indolent, and had not troubled himself to make inquiries. He took her on her own representation as the widow of a merchant who had failed in business.

On the impulse of the moment - an impulse which he could not explain - Carl asked abruptly - "Is your name Cook?"

A look of surprise, almost of stupefaction, appeared on the man's face.

"Who told you my name?" he asked.

"Then your name is Cook?"

"What is your object in asking?" said the man, suspiciously.

"I mean you no harm," returned Carl, "but I have reasons for asking."

"Did you ever see me before?" asked the man.

"No."

"Then what makes you think my name is Cook? It is not written on my face, is it?"

"No."

"Then how -"

Carl interrupted him.

"I know a boy named Peter Cook," he said, "who resembles you very strongly."

"You know Peter Cook - little Peter?" exclaimed the tramp.

"Yes. Is he a relation of yours?"

"I should think so!" responded Cook, emphatically. "He is my own son - that is, if he is a boy of about your age."

"Yes."

"Where is he? Is his mother alive?"

"Your wife!" exclaimed Carl, overwhelmed at the thought.

"She was my wife!" said Cook, "but while I was in California, some years since, she took possession of my small property, procured a divorce through an unprincipled lawyer, and I returned to find myself without wife, child or money. Wasn't that a mean trick?"

"I think it was."

"Can you tell me where she is?" asked Cook, eagerly.

"Yes, I can."

"Where can I find my wife?" asked Cook, with much eagerness.

Carl hesitated. He did not like his stepmother; he felt that she had treated him meanly, but he was not prepared to reveal her present residence till he knew what course Cook intended to pursue.

"She is married again," he said, watching Cook to see what effect this announcement might have upon him.

"I have no objection, I am sure," responded Cook, indifferently. "Did she marry well?"

"She married a man in good circumstances."

"She would take good care of that."

"Then you don't intend to reclaim her?"

"How can I? She obtained a divorce, though by false representations. I am glad to be rid of her, but I want her to restore the two thousand dollars of which she robbed me. I left my property in her hands, but when she ceased to be my wife she had no right to take possession of it. I ought not to be surprised, however. It wasn't the first theft she had committed."

"Can this be true?" asked Carl, excited.

"Yes, I married her without knowing much of her antecedents. Two years after marriage I ascertained that she had served a year's term of imprisonment for a theft of jewelry from a lady with whom she was living as housekeeper."

"Are you sure of this?"

"Certainly. She was recognized by a friend of mine, who had been an official at the prison. When taxed with it by me she admitted it, but claimed that she was innocent. I succeeded in finding a narrative of the trial in an old file of papers, and came to the conclusion that she was justly convicted."

"What did you do?"

"I proposed separation, but she begged me to keep the thing secret, and let ourselves remain the same as before. I agreed out of consideration for her, but had occasion to regret it. My business becoming slack, I decided to go to California in the hope of acquiring a competence. I was not fortunate there, and was barely able, after a year, to get home. I found that my wife had procured a divorce, and appropriated the little money I had left. Where she had gone, or where she had conveyed our son, I could not learn. You say you know where she is."

"I do."

"Will you tell me?"

"Mr. Cook," said Carl, after a pause for reflection, "I will tell you, but not just at present. I am on my way to Chicago on business. On my return I will stop here, and take you with me to the present home of your former wife. You will understand my interest in the matter when I tell you that she is now married to a relative of my own."

"I pity him whoever he is," said Cook.

"Yes, I think he is to be pitied," said Carl, gravely; "but the revelation you will be able to make will enable him to insist upon a separation."

"The best thing he can do! How long before you return to Albany?"

"A week or ten days."

"I don't know how I am to live in the meantime," said Cook, anxiously. "I am penniless, but for the money you have just given me."

"At what price can you obtain board?"

"I know of a decent house where I can obtain board and a small room for five dollars a week."

"Here are twelve dollars. This will pay for two weeks' board, and give you a small sum besides. What is the address?"

Cook mentioned a number on a street by the river.

Carl took it down in a notebook with which he had provided himself.

"When I return to Albany," he said, "I will call there at once."

"You won't forget me?"

"No; I shall be even more anxious to meet you than you will be to meet me. The one to whom your former wife is married is very near and dear to me, and I cannot bear to think that he has been so wronged and imposed upon!"

"Very well, sir! I shall wait for you with confidence. If I can get back from my former wife the money she robbed me of, I can get on my feet again, and take a respectable position in society. It is very hard for a man dressed as I am to obtain any employment."

Looking at his shabby and ragged suit, Carl could readily believe this statement. If he had wished to employ anyone he would hardly have been tempted to engage a man so discreditable in appearance. "Be of good courage, Mr. Cook," he said, kindly. "If your story is correct, and I believe it is, there are better days in store for you."

"Thank you for those words," said Cook, earnestly. "They give me new hope."

Horatio Alger, Jr.

CHAPTER XXXIII.

FROM ALBANY TO NIAGARA.

Carl took the afternoon train on the following day for Buffalo. His thoughts were busy with the startling discovery he had made in regard to his stepmother. Though he had never liked her, he had been far from imagining that she was under the ban of the law. It made him angry to think that his father had been drawn into a marriage with such a woman - that the place of his idolized mother had been taken by one who had served a term at Sing Sing.

Did Peter know of his mother's past disgrace? he asked himself. Probably not, for it had come before his birth. He only wondered that the secret had never got out before. There must be many persons who had known her as a prisoner, and could identify her now. She had certainly been fortunate with the fear of discovery always haunting her. Carl could not understand how she could carry her head so high, and attempt to tyrannize over his father and himself.

What the result would be when Dr. Crawford learned the antecedents of the woman whom he called wife Carl did not for a moment doubt. His father was a man of very strict ideas on the subject of honor, and good repute, and the discovery would lead him to turn from

Mrs. Crawford in abhorrence. Moreover, he was strongly opposed to divorce, and Carl had heard him argue that a divorced person should not be permitted to remarry. Yet in ignorance he had married a divorced woman, who had been convicted of theft, and served a term of imprisonment. The discovery would be a great shock to him, and it would lead to a separation and restore the cordial relations between himself and his son.

Not long after his settlement in Milford; Carl had written as follows to his father:

"Dear Father: - Though I felt obliged to leave home for reasons which we both understand, I am sure that you will feel interested to know how I am getting along. I did not realize till I had started out how difficult it is for a boy, brought up like myself, to support himself when thrown upon his own exertions. A newsboy can generally earn enough money to maintain himself in the style to which he is accustomed, but I have had a comfortable and even luxurious home, and could hardly bring myself to live in a tenement house, or a very cheap boarding place. Yet I would rather do either than stay in a home made unpleasant by the persistent hostility of one member.

"I will not take up your time by relating the incidents of the first two days after I left home. I came near getting into serious trouble through no fault of my own, but happily escaped. When I was nearly penniless I fell in with a prosperous manufacturer of furniture who has taken me into his employment. He gives me a home in his own house, and pays me two dollars a week besides. This is enough to support me econo-mically, and I shall after a while receive better pay.

"I am not in the office, but in the factory, and am learning the business practically, starting in at the bottom. I think I have a taste for it, and the super-intendent tells me I am making remarkable progress. The time was when I would have hesitated to become a working boy, but I have quite got over such foolish-ness. Mr. Jennings, my employer, who is considered a rich man, began as I did, and I hope some day to occupy a position similar to his.

"I trust you are quite well and happy, dear father. My only regret is, that I cannot see you occasionally. While my stepmother and Peter form part of your family, I feel that I can never live at home. They both dislike me, and I am afraid I return the feeling. If you are sick or need me, do not fail to send for me, for I can never forget that you are my father, as I am your affectionate son,

Carl."

This letter was handed to Dr. Crawford at the breakfast table. He colored and looked agitated when he opened the envelope, and Mrs. Crawford, who had a large share of curiosity, did not fail to notice this.

"From whom is your letter, my dear?" she asked, in the soft tone which was habitual with her when she addressed her husband

"The handwriting is Carl's," answered Dr. Crawford, already devouring the letter eagerly.

"Oh!" she answered, in a chilly tone. "I have been

expecting you would hear from him. How much money does he send for?"

"I have not finished the letter." Dr. Crawford continued reading. When he had finished he laid it down beside his plate.

"Well?" said his wife, interrogatively. "What does he have to say? Does he ask leave to come home?"

"No; he is quite content where he is."

"And where is that?"

"At Milford."

"That is not far away?"

"No; not more than sixty miles."

"Does he ask for money?"

"No; he is employed."

"Where?"

"In a furniture factory."

"Oh, a factory boy."

"Yes; he is learning the business."

"He doesn't seem to be very ambitious," sneered Mrs. Crawford.

"On the contrary, he is looking forward to being in

Horatio Alger, Jr.

business for himself some day."

"On your money - I understand."

"Really, Mrs. Crawford, you do the boy injustice. He hints nothing of the kind. He evidently means to raise himself gradually as his employer did before him. By the way, he has a home in his employer's family. I think Mr. Jennings must have taken a fancy to Carl."

"I hope he will find him more agreeable than I did," said Mrs. Crawford, sharply.

"Are you quite sure that you always treated Carl considerately, my dear?"

"I didn't flatter or fondle him, if that is what you mean. I treated him as well as he could expect."

"Did you treat him as well as Peter, for example?"

"No. There is a great difference between the two boys. Peter is always respectful and obliging, and doesn't set up his will against mine. He never gives me a moment's uneasiness."

"I hope you will continue to find him a comfort, my dear," said Dr. Crawford, meekly.

He looked across the table at the fat, expressionless face of his stepson, and he blamed himself because he could not entertain a warmer regard for Peter. Somehow he had a slight feeling of antipathy, which he tried to overcome.

"No doubt he is a good boy, since his mother says so,"

reflected the doctor, "but I don't appreciate him. I will take care, however, that neither he nor his mother sees this."

When Peter heard his mother's encomium upon him, he laughed in his sleeve.

"I'll remind ma of that when she scolds me," he said to himself. "I'm glad Carl isn't coming back. He was always interferin' with me. Now, if ma and I play our cards right we'll get all his father's money. Ma thinks he won't live long, I heard her say so the other day. Won't it be jolly for ma and me to come into a fortune, and live just as we please! I hope ma will go to New York. It's stupid here, but I s'pose we'll have to stay for the present."

"Is Carl's letter private?" asked Mrs. Crawford, after a pause.

"I - I think he would rather I didn't show it ," returned her husband, remembering the allusion made by Carl to his stepmother.

"Oh, well, I am not curious," said Mrs. Crawford, tossing her head.

None the less, however, she resolved to see and read the letter, if she could get hold of it without her husband's knowledge. He was so careless that she did not doubt soon to find it laid down somewhere. In this she proved correct. Before the day was over, she found Carl's letter in her husband's desk. She opened and read it eagerly with a running fire of comment.

"'Reasons which we both understand,'" she repeated,

scornfully. "That is a covert attack upon me. Of course, I ought to expect that. So he had a hard time. Well, it served him right for conducting himself as he did. Ah, here is another hit at me - `Yet I would rather do either than live in a home made unpleasant by the persistent hostility of one member.' He is trying to set his father against me. Well, he won't succeed. I can twist Dr. Paul Crawford round my finger, luckily, and neither his son nor anyone else can diminish my influence over him."

She read on for some time till she reached this passage: "While my stepmother and Peter form a part of your family I can never live at home. They both dislike me, and I am afraid I return the feeling." "Thanks for the information," she muttered. "I knew it before. This letter doesn't make me feel any more friendly to you, Carl Crawford. I see that you are trying to ingratiate yourself with your father, and prejudice him against me and my poor Peter, but I think I can defeat your kind intentions."

She folded up the letter, and replaced it in her husband's desk.

"I wonder if my husband will answer Carl's artful epistle," she said to herself. "He can if he pleases. He is weak as water, and I will see that he goes no farther than words."

Dr. Crawford did answer Carl's letter. This is his reply:

"Dear Carl: - i am glad to hear that you are comfortably situated. I regret that you were so headstrong and unreasonable. It seems to me that you might, with a little effort, have got on with your stepmother. You could hardly expect her to treat you in the same way as her own son. He seems to be a good boy, but I own that I have never been able to become attached to him."

Carl read this part of the letter with satisfaction. He knew how mean and contemptible Peter was, and it would have gone to his heart to think that his father had transferred his affection to the boy he had so much reason to dislike.

"I am glad you are pleased with your prospects. I think I could have done better for you had your relations with your stepmother been such as to make it pleasant for you to remain at home. You are right in thinking that I am interested in your welfare. I hope, my dear Carl, you will become a happy and prosperous man. I do not forget that you are my son, and I am still your affectionate father,

"Paul Crawford."

Carl was glad to receive this letter. It showed him that his stepmother had not yet succeeded in alienating from him his father's affection.

But we must return to the point where we left Carl on his journey to Buffalo. He enjoyed his trip over the Central road during the hours of daylight. He determined on his return to make an all-day trip so that he might enjoy the scenery through which he now rode in the darkness.

At Buffalo he had no other business except that of Mr. Jennings, and immediately after breakfast he began to make a tour of the furniture establishments. He met with excellent success, and had the satisfaction of sending home some large orders. In the evening he took train for Niagara, wishing to see the falls in the early morning, and resume his journey in the afternoon.

He registered at the International Hotel on the American side. It was too late to do more than take an evening walk, and see the falls gleaming like silver through the darkness.

"I will go to bed early," thought Carl, "and get up at six o'clock."

He did go to bed early, but he was more fatigued than he supposed, and slept longer than he anticipated. It was eight o'clock before he came downstairs. Before going in to breakfast, he took a turn on the piazzas. Here he fell in with a sociable gentleman, much addicted to gossip.

"Good-morning!" he said. "Have you seen the falls yet?"

"I caught a glimpse of them last evening I am going to visit them after breakfast."

"There are a good many people staying here just now - some quite noted persons, too."

"Indeed!"

"Yes, what do you say to an English lord?" and Carl's new friend nodded with am important air, as if it reflected great credit on the hotel to have so important a guest.

"Does he look different from anyone else?" asked Carl, smiling.

"Well, to tell the truth, he isn't much to look at," said the other. "The gentleman who is with him looks more stylish. I thought he was the lord at first, but I afterwards learned that he was an American named Stuyvesant."

Carl started at the familiar name.

"Is he tall and slender, with side whiskers, and does he wear eyeglasses?" he asked, eagerly.

"Yes; you know him then?" said the other, in surprise.

"Yes," answered Carl, with a smile, "I am slightly acquainted with him. I am very anxious to meet him again."

CHAPTER XXXIV.

CARL MAKES THE ACQUAINTANCE
OF AN ENGLISH LORD.

"There they are now," said the stranger, suddenly pointing out two persons walking slowly along the piazza. "The small man, in the rough suit, and mutton-chop whiskers, is Lord Bedford."

Carl eyed the British nobleman with some curiosity. Evidently Lord Bedford was no dude. His suit was of rough cloth and illfitting. He was barely five feet six inches in height, with features decidedly plain, but with an absence of pretension that was creditable to him, considering that he was really what he purported to be. Stuyvesant walked by his side, nearly a head taller, and of more distinguished bearing, though of plebeian extraction. His manner was exceedingly deferential, and he was praising England and everything English in a fulsome manner.

"Yes, my lord," Carl overheard him say, "I have often thought that society in England is far superior to our American society."

"Thanks, you are very kind," drawled the nobleman, "but really I find things very decent in America, upon my word. I had been reading Dickens's `Notes' before I came over and I expected to find you very uncivilized, and - almost aboriginal; but I assure you I have met some very gentlemanly persons in America, some almost up to our English standard."

"Really, my lord, such a tribute from a man in your position is most gratifying. May I state this on your authority?"

"Yes, I don't mind, but I would rather not get into the papers, don't you know. You are not a - reporter, I hope."

"I hope not," said Mr. Stuyvesant, in a lofty tone. "I am a scion of one of the oldest families in New York. Of course I know that social position is a very different thing here from what it is in England. It must be a gratifying thing to reflect that you are a lord."

"Yes, I suppose so. I never thought much about it."

"I should like so much to be a lord. I care little for money."

"Then, by Jove, you are a remarkable man."

"In comparison with rank, I mean. I would rather be a lord with a thousand pounds a year than a rich merchant with ten times as much."

"You'll find it very inconvenient being a lord on a thousand; you might as well be a beggar."

"I suppose, of course, high rank requires a large rent roll. In fact, a New York gentleman requires more than a trifle to support him. I can't dress on less than two hundred pounds a year."

"Your American tailors are high-priced, then?"

"Those that I employ; we have cheap tailors, of course, but I generally go to Bell."

Mr. Stuyvesant was posing as a gentleman of fashion. Carl, who followed at a little distance behind the pair, was much amused by his remarks, knowing what he did about him.

"I think a little of going to England in a few months," continued Stuyvesant.

"Indeed! You must look me up," said Bedford, carelessly.

"I should, indeed, be delighted," said Stuyvesant, effusively.

"That is, if I am in England. I may be on the Continent, but you can inquire for me at my club - the Piccadilly."

"I shall esteem it a great honor, my lord. I have a penchant for good society. The lower orders are not attractive to me."

"They are sometimes more interesting," said the Englishman; "but do you know, I am surprised to hear an American speak in this way. I thought you were all on a level here in a republic."

"Oh, my lord!" expostulated Stuyvesant, deprecatingly. "You don't think I would associate with shopkeepers and common tradesmen?"

"I don't know. A cousin of mine is interested in a wine business in London. He is a younger son with a small fortune, and draws a very tidy income from his city business."

"But his name doesn't appear on the sign, I infer."

"No, I think not. Then you are not in business, Mr. Stuyvesant?"

"No; I inherited an income from my father. It isn't as large as I could wish, and I have abstained from marrying because I could not maintain the mode of living to which I have been accustomed."

"You should marry a rich girl."

"True! I may do so, since your lordship recommends it. In fact, I have in view a young lady whose father was once lord mayor (I beg pardon, mayor) of New York. Her father is worth a million."

"Pounds?"

"Well, no, dollars. I should have said two hundred thousand pounds."

"If the girl is willing, it may be a good plan."

"Thank you, my lord. Your advice is very kind."

"The young man seems on very good terms with Lord Bedford," said Carl's companion, whose name was Atwood, with a shade of envy in his voice.

"Yes," said Carl.

Horatio Alger, Jr.

"I wish he would introduce me," went on Mr. Atwood.

"I should prefer the introduction of a different man," said Carl.

"Why? He seems to move in good society."

"Without belonging to it."

"Then you know him?"

"Better than I wish I did."

Atwood looked curious.

"I will explain later," said Carl; "now I must go in to breakfast."

"I will go with you."

Though Stuyvesant had glanced at Carl, he did not appear to recognize him, partly, no doubt, because he had no expectation of meeting the boy he had robbed, at Niagara. Besides, his time and attention were so much taken up by his aristocratic acquaintance that he had little notice for anyone else. Carl observed with mingled amusement and vexation that Mr. Stuyvesant wore a new necktie, which he had bought for himself in New York, and which had been in the stolen gripsack.

"If I can find Lord Bedford alone I will put him on his guard," thought Carl. "I shall spoil Mr. Stuyvesant's plans."

After breakfast Carl prepared to go down to the falls.

On the way he overtook Lord Bedford walking in the same direction, and, as it happened, without a companion. Carl quickened his pace, and as he caught up with him, he raised his hat, and said: "Lord Bedford, I believe."

"Yes," answered the Englishman, inquiringly.

"I must apologize for addressing a stranger, but I want to put you on your guard against a young man whom I saw walking with you on the piazza."

"Is he - what do you know of him?" asked Lord Bedford, laying aside his air of indifference.

"I know that he is an adventurer and a thief. I made his acquaintance on a Hudson River steamer, and he walked off with my valise and a small sum of money."

"Is this true?" asked the Englishman, in amazement.

"Quite true. He is wearing one of my neckties at this moment."

"The confounded cad!" ejaculated the Englishman, angrily. "I suppose he intended to rob me."

"I have no doubt of it. That is why I ventured to put you on your guard."

"I am a thousand times obliged to you. Why, the fellow told me he belonged to one of the best families in New York."

"If he does, he doesn't do much credit to the family."

"Quite true! Why, he was praising everything English. He evidently wanted to gain my confidence."

"May I ask where you met him?" asked Carl.

"On the train. He offered me a light. Before I knew it, he was chatting familiarly with me. But his game is spoiled. I will let him know that I see through him and his designs." "Then my object is accomplished," said Carl. "Please excuse my want of ceremony." He turned to leave, but Bedford called him back.

"If you are going to the falls, remain with me," he said. "We shall enjoy it better in company."

"With pleasure. Let me introduce myself as Carl Crawford. I am traveling on business and don't belong to one of the first families."

"I see you will suit me," said the Englishman, smiling.

Just then up came Stuyvesant, panting and breathless. "My lord," he said, "I lost sight of you. If you will allow me I will join you.

"Sir!" said the Englishman, in a freezing voice, "I have not the honor of knowing you."

Stuyvesant was overwhelmed.

"I - I hope I have not offended you, my lord," he said.

"Sir, I have learned your character from this young man."

This called the attention of Stuyvesant to Carl. He

flushed as he recognized him

"Mr. Stuyvesant," said Carl, "I must trouble you to return the valise you took from my stateroom, and the pocketbook which you borrowed. My name is Carl Crawford, and my room is 71."

Stuyvesant turned away abruptly. He left the valise at the desk, but Carl never recovered his money.

Horatio Alger, Jr.

CHAPTER XXXV.

WHAT CARL LEARNED IN CHICAGO.

As Carl walked back from the falls he met Mr. Atwood, who was surprised to find h*is young acquaintance on such intimate terms with Lord Bedford. He was about to pass with a bow, when Carl, who was good-natured, said: "Won't you join us, Mr. Atwood? If Lord Bedford will permit, I should like to introduce you."

"Glad to know any friend of yours, Mr. Crawford," said the Englishman, affably.

"I feel honored by the introduction," said Atwood, bowing profoundly.

"I hope you are not a friend of Mr. - ah, Mr. Stuyvesant," said the nobleman, "the person I was talking with this morning. Mr. Crawford tells me he is a - what do you call it? - a confidence man."

"I have no acquaintance with him, my lord. I saw him just now leaving the hotel."

"I am afraid he has gone away with my valise and money," said Carl.

"If you should be inconvenienced, Mr. Crawford," said the nobleman, "my purse is at your disposal."

"Thank you very much, Lord Bedford," said Carl, gratefully. "I am glad to say I am still fairly well provided with money."

"I was about to make you the same offer, Mr. Crawford," said Atwood.

"Thank you! I appreciate your kindness, even if I'm not obliged to avail myself of it."

Returning to the hotel, Lord Bedford ordered a carriage, and invited Atwood and Carl to accompany him on a drive. Mr. Atwood was in an ecstasy, and anticipated with proud satisfaction telling his family of his intimate friend, Lord Bedford, of England. The peer, though rather an ordinary-looking man, seemed to him a model of aristocratic beauty. It was a weakness on the part of Mr. Atwood, but an amiable one, and is shared by many who live under republican institutions.

After dinner Carl felt obliged to resume his journey. He had found his visit to Niagara very agreeable, but his was a business and not a pleasure trip, and loyalty to his employer required him to cut it short. Lord Bedford shook his hand heartily at parting.

"I hope we shall meet again, Mr. Crawford," he said. "I expect, myself, to reach Chicago on Saturday, and shall be glad to have you call on me at the Palmer House."

"Thank you, my lord; I will certainly inquire for

you there."

"He is a very good fellow, even if he is a lord," thought Carl.

Our young hero was a thorough American, and was disposed to think with Robert Burns, that

> "The rank is but the guinea, stamp; The man's the gold for a' that!"

No incident worth recording befell Carl on his trip to Chicago. As a salesman he met with excellent success, and surprised Mr. Jennings by the size of his orders. He was led, on reaching Chicago, to register at the Sherman House, on Clark Street, one of the most reliable among the many houses for travelers offered by the great Western metropolis.

On the second day he made it a point to find out the store of John French, hoping to acquire the information desired by Miss Norris.

It was a store of good size, and apparently well stocked. Feeling the need of new footgear, Carl entered and asked to be shown some shoes. He was waited upon by a young clerk named Gray, with whom he struck up a pleasant acquaintance.

"Do you live in Chicago?" asked Gray? sociably.

"No; I am from New York State. I am here on business."

"Staying at a hotel?"

"Yes, at the Sherman. If you are at leisure this evening I shall be glad to have you call on me. I am a stranger here, and likely to find the time hang heavy on my hands."

"I shall be free at six o'clock."

"Then come to supper with me."

"Thank you, I shall be glad to do so," answered Gray, with alacrity. Living as he did at a cheap boarding house, the prospect of a supper at a first-class hotel was very attractive. He was a pleasant-faced young man of twenty, who had drifted to Chicago from his country home in Indiana, and found it hard to make both ends meet on a salary of nine dollars a week. His habits were good, his manner was attractive and won him popularity with customer's, and with patience he was likely to succeed in the end.

"I wish I could live like this every day," he said, as he rose from a luxurious supper. "At present my finances won't allow me to board at the Sherman."

"Nor would mine," said Carl; "but I am allowed to spend money more freely when I am traveling."

"Are you acquainted in New York?" asked Gray.

"I have little or no acquaintance in the city," answered Carl.

"I should be glad to get a position there."

"Are you not satisfied with your present place?"

"I am afraid I shall not long keep it."

"Why not? Do you think you are in any danger of being discharged?"

"It is not that. I am afraid Mr. French will be obliged to give up business."

"Why?" asked Carl, with keen interest.

"I have reason to think he is embarrassed. I know that he has a good many bills out, some of which have been running a long time. If any pressure is brought to bear upon him, he may have to suspend."

Carl felt that he was obtaining important information. If Mr. French were in such a condition Miss Norris would be pretty sure to lose her money if she advanced it.

"To what do you attribute Mr. French's embarrassment?" he asked.

"He lives expensively in a handsome house near Lincoln Park, and draws heavily upon the business for his living expenses. I think that explains it. I only wonder that he has been able to hold out so long."

"Perhaps if he were assisted he would be able to keep his head above water."

"He would need a good deal of assistance. You see that my place isn't very secure, and I shall soon need to be looking up another."

"I don't think I shall need to inquire any farther,"

thought Carl. "It seems to me Miss Norris had better keep her money."

Before he retired he indited the following letter to his Albany employer:

Miss Rachel Norris.

"Dear Madam: - I have attended to your commission, and have to report that Mr. French appears to be involved in business embarrassments, and in great danger to bankruptcy. The loan he asks of you would no doubt be of service, but probably would not long delay the crash. If you wish to assist him, it would be better to allow him to fail, and then advance him the money to put him on his feet. I am told that his troubles come from living beyond his means.

"Yours respectfully,
"Carl Crawford."

By return mail Carl received the following note:

"My Dear Young Friend: - Your report confirms the confidence I reposed in you. It is just the information I desired. I shall take your advice and refuse the loan. What other action I may take hereafter I cannot tell. When you return, should you stop in Albany, please call on me. If unable to do this, write me from Milford.

Your friend,
"Rachel Norris."

Carl was detained for several days in Chicago. He

Horatio Alger, Jr.

chanced to meet his English friend, Lord Bedford, upon his arrival, and the nobleman, on learning where he was staying, also registered at the Sherman House. In his company Carl took a drive over the magnificent boulevard which is the pride of Chicago, and rose several degrees in the opinion of those guests who noticed his intimacy with the English guest.

Carl had just completed his Chicago business when, on entering the hotel, he was surprised to see a neighbor of his father's - Cyrus Robinson - a prominent business man of Edgewood Center. Carl was delighted, for he had not been home, or seen any home friends for over a year.

"I am glad to see you, Mr. Robinson," he said, offering his hand.

"What! Carl Crawford!" exclaimed Robinson, in amazement. "How came you in Chicago? Your father did not tell me you were here."

"He does not know it. I am only here on a business visit. Tell me, Mr. Robinson, how is my father?"

"I think, Carl, that he is not at all well. I am quite sure he misses you, and I don't believe your stepmother's influence over him is beneficial. Just before I came away I heard a rumor that troubled me. It is believed in Edgewood that she is trying to induce your father to make a will leaving all, or nearly all his property to her and her son."

"I don't care so much for that, Mr. Robinson, as for my father's health."

"Carl," said Robinson, significantly, "if such a will is made I don't believe your father will live long after it."

"You don't mean that?" said Carl, horror-struck.

"I think Mrs. Crawford, by artful means will worry your father to death. He is of a nervous temperament, and an unscrupulous woman can shorten his life without laying herself open to the law."

Carl's face grew stern.

"I will save my father," he said, "and defeat my stepmother's wicked schemes."

"I pray Heaven you can. There is no time to be lost."

"I shall lose no time, you may be sure. I shall be at Edgewood within a week."

CHAPTER XXXVI.

MAKING A WILL.

In Edgewood Center events moved slowly. In Carl Crawford's home dullness reigned supreme. He had been the life of the house, and his absence, though welcome to his stepmother, was seriously felt by his father, who day by day became thinner and weaker, while his step grew listless and his face seldom brightened with a smile. He was anxious to have Carl at home again, and the desire became so strong that he finally broached the subject.

"My dear," he said one day at the breakfast table, "I have been thinking of Carl considerably of late."

"Indeed!" said Mrs. Crawford, coldly.

"I think I should like to have him at home once more."

Mrs. Crawford smiled ominously.

"He is better off where he is," she said, softly.

"But he is my only son, and I never see him," pleaded her husband.

"You know very well, Dr. Crawford," rejoined his

wife, "that your son only made trouble in the house while he was here."

"Yet it seems hard that he should be driven from his father's home, and forced to take refuge among strangers."

"I don't know what you mean by his being driven from home," said Mrs. Crawford, tossing her head. "He made himself disagreeable, and, not being able to have his own way, he took French leave."

"The house seems very lonely without him," went on Dr. Crawford, who was too wise to get into an argument with his wife.

"It certainly is more quiet. As for company, Peter is still here, and would at any time stay with you."

Peter did not relish this suggestion, and did not indorse it.

"I should not care to confine him to the house," said Dr. Crawford, as his glance rested on the plain and by no means agreeable face of his stepson.

"I suppose I need not speak of myself. You know that you can always call upon me."

If Dr. Crawford had been warmly attached to his second wife, this proposal would have cheered him, but the time had gone by when he found any pleasure in her society. There was a feeling of almost repulsion which he tried to conceal, and he was obliged to acknowledge to himself that the presence of his wife gave him rather uneasiness than comfort.

Horatio Alger, Jr.

"Carl is very well off where he is," resumed Mrs. Crawford. "He is filling a business position, humble, perhaps, but still one that gives him his living and keeps him out of mischief. Let well enough alone, doctor, and don't interrupt his plans."

"I - I may be foolish," said the doctor, hesitating, "but I have not been feeling as well as usual lately, and if anything should happen to me while Carl was absent I should die very unhappy."

Mrs. Crawford regarded her husband with uneasiness.

"Do you mean that you think you are in any danger?" she asked.

"I don't know. I am not an old man, but, on the other hand, I am an invalid. My father died when he was only a year older than I am at present."

Mrs. Crawford drew out her handkerchief, and proceeded to wipe her tearless eyes.

"You distress me beyond measure by your words, my dear husband. How can I think of your death without emotion? What should I do without you?"

"My dear, you must expect to survive me. You are younger than I, and much stronger."

"Besides," and Mrs. Crawford made an artful pause, "I hardly like to mention it, but Peter and I are poor, and by your death might be left to the cold mercies of the world."

"Surely I would not fail to provide for you."

Mrs. Crawford shook her head.

"I am sure of your kind intentions, my husband," she said, "but they will not avail unless you provide for me in your will."

"Yes, it's only right that I should do so. As soon as I feel equal to the effort I will draw up a will."

"I hope you will, for I should not care to be dependent on Carl, who does not like me. I hope you will not think me mercenary, but to Peter and myself this is of vital importance."

"No, I don't misjudge you. I ought to have thought of it before."

"I don't care so much about myself," said Mrs. Crawford, in a tone of self-sacrifice, "but I should not like to have Peter thrown upon the world without means."

"All that you say is wise and reasonable," answered her husband, wearily. "I will attend to the matter to-morrow."

The next day Mrs. Crawford came into her husband's presence with a sheet of legal cap.

"My dear husband," she said, in a soft, insinuating tone, "I wished to spare you trouble, and I have accordingly drawn up a will to submit to you, and receive your signature, if you approve it."

Dr. Crawford looked surprised.

"Where did you learn to write a will?" he asked.

"I used in my days of poverty to copy documents for a lawyer," she replied. "In this way I became something of a lawyer myself."

"I see. Will you read what you have prepared?"

Mrs. Crawford read the document in her hand. It provided in the proper legal phraseology for an equal division of the testator's estate between the widow and Carl.

"I didn't know, of course, what provision you intended to make for me," she said, meekly. "Perhaps you do not care to leave me half the estate."

"Yes, that seems only fair. You do not mention Peter. I ought to do something for him."

"Your kindness touches me, my dear husband, but I shall be able to provide for him out of my liberal bequest. I do not wish to rob your son, Carl. I admit that I do not like him, but that shall not hinder me from being just."

Dr. Crawford was pleased with this unexpected concession from his wife. He felt that he should be more at ease if Carl's future was assured.

"Very well, my dear," he said, cheerfully. "I approve of the will as you have drawn it up, and I will affix my signature at once." "Then, shall I send for two of the neighbors to witness it?"

"It will be well."

Two near neighbors were sent for and witnessed Dr. Crawford's signature to the will.

There was a strangely triumphant look in Mrs. Crawford's eyes as she took the document after it had been duly executed.

"You will let me keep this, doctor?" she asked. "It will be important for your son as well as myself, that it should be in safe hands."

"Yes; I shall be glad to have you do so. I rejoice that it is off my mind."

"You won't think me mercenary, my dear husband, or indifferent to your life?"

"No; why should I?"

"Then I am satisfied."

Mrs. Crawford took the will, and carrying it upstairs, opened her trunk, removed the false bottom, and deposited under it the last will and testament of Dr. Paul Crawford.

"At last!" she said to herself. "I am secure, and have compassed what I have labored for so long."

Dr. Crawford had not noticed that the will to which he affixed his signature was not the same that had been read to him. Mrs. Crawford had artfully substituted another paper of quite different tenor. By the will actually executed, the entire estate was left to Mrs. Crawford, who was left guardian of her son and Carl, and authorized to make such provision for each as she might deem suitable. This, of course, made Carl entirely dependent on a woman who hated him.

"Now, Dr. Paul Crawford," said Mrs. Crawford to herself, with a cold smile, "you may die as soon as you please. Peter and I are provided for. Your father died when a year older than you are now, you tell me. It is hardly likely that you will live to a greater age than he."

She called the next day on the family physician, and with apparent solicitude asked his opinion of Dr. Crawford's health.

"He is all I have," she said, pathetically, "all except my dear Peter. Tell me what you think of his chances of continued life."

"Your husband," replied the physician, "has one weak organ. It is his heart. He may live for fifteen or twenty years, but a sudden excitement might carry him off in a moment. The best thing you can do for him is to keep him tranquil and free from any sudden shock."

Mrs. Crawford listened attentively.

"I will do my best," she said, "since so much depends on it."

When she returned home it was with a settled purpose in her heart.

CHAPTER XXXVII.

PETER LETS OUT A SECRET.

"Can you direct me to the house of Dr. Crawford?" asked a stranger.

The inquiry was addressed to Peter Cook in front of the hotel in Edgewood Center.

"Yes, sir; he is my stepfather!"

"Indeed! I did not know that my old friend was married again. You say you are his stepson?"

"Yes, sir."

"He has an own son, about your age, I should judge."

"That's Carl! he is a little older than me."

"Is he at home?"

"No," answered Peter, pursing up his lips.

"Is he absent at boarding school?"

"No; he's left home."

"Indeed!" ejaculated the stranger, in surprise. "How is that?"

"He was awfully hard to get along with, and didn't treat mother with any respect. He wanted to have his own way, and, of course, ma couldn't stand that."

"I see," returned the stranger, and he eyed Peter curiously. "What did his father say to his leaving home?" he asked.

"Oh, he always does as ma wishes."

"Was Carl willing to leave home?"

"Yes; he said he would rather go than obey ma."

"I suppose he receives an allowance from his father?"

"No; he wanted one, but ma put her foot down and said he shouldn't have one."

"Your mother seems to be a woman of considerable firmness."

"You bet, she's firm. She don't allow no boy to boss her."

"Really, this boy is a curiosity," said Reuben Ashcroft to himself. "He doesn't excel in the amiable and attractive qualities. He has a sort of brutal frankness which can't keep a secret."

"How did you and Carl get along together?" he asked, aloud.

"We didn't get along at all. He wanted to boss me, and ma and I wouldn't have it."

"So the upshot was that he had to leave the house and you remained?"

"Yes, that's the way of it," said Peter, laughing.

"And Carl was actually sent out to earn his own living without help of any kind from his father?"

"Yes."

"What is he doing?" asked Ashcroft, in some excitement. "Good heavens! he may have suffered from hunger."

"Are you a friend of his?" asked Peter, sharply.

"I am a friend of anyone who requires a friend."

"Carl is getting along well enough. He is at work in some factory in Milford, and gets a living."

"Hasn't he been back since he first left home?"

"No."

"How long ago is that?"

"Oh, 'bout a year," answered Peter, carelessly.

"How is Dr. Crawford? Is he in good health?"

"He ain't very well. Ma told me the other day she didn't think he would live long. She got him to make a will the other day."

"Why, this seems to be a conspiracy!" thought Ashcroft. "I'd give something to see that will."

"I suppose he will provide for you and your mother handsomely?"

"Yes; ma said she was to have control of the property. I guess Carl will have to stand round if he expects any favors."

"It is evident this boy can't keep a secret," thought Ashcroft. "All the better for me. I hope I am in time to defeat this woman's schemes."

"There's the house," said Peter, pointing it out.

"Do you think Dr. Crawford is at home?"

"Oh, yes, he doesn't go out much. Ma is away this afternoon. She's at the sewing circle, I think."

"Thank you for serving as my guide," said Ashcroft. "There's a little acknowledgment which I hope will be of service to you."

He offered a half dollar to Peter, who accepted it joyfully and was profuse in his thanks.

"Now, if you will be kind enough to tell the doctor that an old friend wishes to see him, I shall be still further obliged."

"Just follow me, then," said Peter, and he led the way into the sitting-room.

CHAPTER XXXVIII.

Dr. CRAWFORD IS TAKEN TO TASK.

After the first greetings, Reuben Ashcroft noticed with pain the fragile look of his friend.

"Are you well?" he asked

"I am not very strong," said Dr. Crawford, smiling faintly, "but Mrs. Crawford takes good care of me."

"And Carl, too - he is no doubt a comfort to you?"

Dr. Crawford flushed painfully.

"Carl has been away from home for a year, he said, with an effort.

"That is strange your own son, too! Is there anything unpleasant? You may confide in me, as I am the cousin of Carl's mother.'

"The fact is, Carl and Mrs. Crawford didn't hit it off very well."

"And you took sides against your own son, said Ashcroft, indignantly.

Horatio Alger, Jr.

"I begin to think I was wrong, Reuben. You don't know how I have missed the boy."

"Yet you sent him out into the world without a penny."

"How do you know that?" asked Dr. Crawford quickly.

"I had a little conversation with your stepson as I came to the house. He spoke very frankly and unreservedly about family affairs; He says you do whatever his mother tells you.

Dr. Crawford looked annoyed and blushed with shame.

"Did he say that?" he asked.

"Yes; he said his mother would not allow you to help Carl."

"He - misunderstood "

"Paul, I fear he understands the case only too well. I don't want to pain you, but your wife is counting on your speedy death."

"I told her I didn't think I should live long."

"And she got you to make a will?"

"Yes; did Peter tell you that?"

"He said his mother was to have control of the property, and Carl would get nothing if he didn't act so as to please her."

"There is some mistake here. By my will - made

yesterday - Carl is to have an equal share, and nothing is said about his being dependent on anyone."

"Who drew up the will?"

"Mrs. Crawford."

"Did you read it?"

"Yes."

Ashcroft looked puzzled.

"I should like to read the will myself," he said, after a pause. "Where is it now?"

"Mrs. Crawford has charge of it."

Reuben Ashcroft remained silent, but his mind was busy.

"That woman is a genius of craft," he said to himself. "My poor friend is but a child in her hands. I did not know Paul would be so pitiably weak."

"How do you happen to be here in Edgewood, Reuben?" asked the doctor.

"I had a little errand in the next town, and could not resist the temptation of visiting you."

"You can stay a day or two, can you not?"

"I will, though I had not expected to do so."

"Mrs. Crawford is away this afternoon. She will be

back presently, and then I will introduce you."

At five o'clock Mrs. Crawford returned, and her husband introduced her to his friend.

Ashcroft fixed his eyes upon her searchingly.

"Her face looks strangely familiar," he said to himself. "Where can I have seen her?"

Mrs. Crawford, like all persons who have a secret to conceal, was distrustful of strangers. She took an instant dislike to Reuben Ashcroft, and her greeting was exceedingly cold.

"I have invited Mr. Ashcroft to make me a visit of two or three days, my dear," said her husband. "He is a cousin to Carl's mother."

Mrs. Crawford made no response, but kept her eyes fixed upon the carpet. She could not have shown more plainly that the invitation was not approved by her.

"Madam does not want me here," thought Ashcroft, as he fixed his gaze once more upon his friend's wife. Again the face looked familiar, but he could not place it.

"Have I not seen you before, Mrs. Crawford?" he asked, abruptly.

"I don't remember you," she answered, slowly. "Probably I resemble some one you have met."

"Perhaps so," answered Ashcroft, but he could not get rid of the conviction that somewhere and some time in the past he had met Mrs. Crawford, and under circumstances that had fixed her countenance in his memory.

After supper Dr. Crawford said: "My dear, I have told our guest that I had, as a prudential measure, made my will. I wish you would get it, and let me read it to him."

Mrs. Crawford looked startled and annoyed.

"Couldn't you tell him the provisions of it?" she said.

"Yes, but I should like to show him the document."

She turned and went upstairs. She was absent at least ten minutes. When she returned she was empty-handed.

"I am sorry to say," she remarked, with a forced laugh, "that I have laid away the will so carefully that I can't find it."

Ashcroft fixed a searching look upon her, that evidently annoyed her.

"I may be able to find it to-morrow," she resumed.

"I think you told me, Paul," said Ashcroft, turning to Dr. Crawford, "that by the will your estate is divided equally between Carl and Mrs. Crawford."

"Yes."

"And nothing is said of any guardianship on the part of Mrs. Crawford?"

"No; I think it would be better, Ashcroft, that you should be Carl's guardian. A man can study his interests and control him better."

"I will accept the trust," said Ashcroft, "though I hope it may be many years before the necessity arises."

Mrs. Crawford bit her lips, and darted an angry glance at the two friends. She foresaw that her plans were threatened with failure.

The two men chatted throughout the evening, and Dr. Crawford had never of late seemed happier. It gave him new life and raised his spirits to chat over old times with his early friend.

CHAPTER XXXIX.

A MAN OF ENERGY.

The next morning Ashcroft said to his host: "Paul, let us take a walk to the village."

Dr. Crawford put on his hat, and went out with his friend.

"Now, Paul," said Ashcroft, when they were some rods distant from the house, "is there a lawyer in Edgewood?"

"Certainly, and a good one."

"Did he indite your will?"

"No; Mrs. Crawford wrote it out. She was at one time copyist for a lawyer."

"Take my advice and have another drawn up to-day without mentioning the matter to her. She admits having mislaid the one made yesterday."

"It may be a good idea."

"Certainly, it is a prudent precaution. Then you will be sure that all is safe. I have, myself, executed a

Horatio Alger, Jr.

duplicate will. One I keep, the other I have deposited with my lawyer."

Ashcroft was a man of energy. He saw that Dr. Crawford, who was of a weak, vacillating temper, executed the will. He and another witnessed it, and the document was left with the lawyer.

"You think I had better not mention the matter to Mrs. Crawford?" he said.

"By no means - she might think it was a reflection upon her for carelessly mislaying the first."

"True," and the doctor, who was fond of peace, consented to his friend's plan.

"By the way," asked Ashcroft, "who was your wife what was her name, I mean - before her second marriage?"

"She was a Mrs. Cook."

"Oh, I see," said Ashcroft, and his face lighted up with surprise and intelligence

"What do you see?" inquired Dr. Crawford. "I thought your wife's face was familiar. I met her once when she was Mrs. Cook."

"You knew her, then?"

"No, I never exchanged a word with her till I met her under this roof.

"How can I tell him that I first saw her when a visitor

to the penitentiary among the female prisoners?" Ashcroft asked himself. "My poor friend would sink with mortification."

They were sitting in friendly chat after their return from their walk, when Mrs. Crawford burst into the room in evident excitement.

"Husband," she cried, "Peter has brought home a terrible report. He has heard from a person who has just come from Milford that Carl has been run over on the railroad and instantly killed!"

Dr. Crawford turned pale, his features worked convulsively, and he put his hand to his heart, as he sank back in his chair, his face as pale as the dead.

"Woman!" said Ashcroft, sternly, "I believe you have killed your husband!"

"Oh, don't say that! How could I be so imprudent?" said Mrs. Crawford, clasping her hands, and counterfeiting distress.

Ashcroft set himself at once to save his friend from the result of the shock.

"Leave the room!" he said, sternly, to Mrs. Crawford.

"Why should I? I am his wife."

"And have sought to be his murderer. You know that he has heart disease. Mrs. - Cook, I know more about you than you suppose."

Mrs. Crawford's color receded.

"I don't understand you," she said. She had scarcely reached the door, when there was a sound of footsteps outside and Carl dashed into the room, nearly upsetting his stepmother.

"You here?" she said, frigidly.

"What is the matter with my father?" asked Carl.

"Are you Carl?" said Ashcroft, quickly.

"Yes."

"Your father has had a shock. I think I can soon bring him to."

A few minutes later Dr. Crawford opened his eyes.

"Are you feeling better, Paul?" asked Ashcroft, anxiously.

"Didn't I hear something about Carl - something terrible?"

"Carl is alive and well," said he, soothingly;

"Are you sure of that?" asked Dr. Crawford, in excitement.

"Yes, I have the best evidence of it. Here is Carl himself."

Carl came forward and was clasped in his father's arms.

"Thank Heaven, you are alive," he said.

"Why should I not be?" asked Carl, bewildered, turning to Ashcroft.

"Your stepmother had the - let me say imprudence, to tell your father that you had been killed on the railroad."

"Where could she have heard such a report?"

"I am not sure that she heard it at all," said Ashcroft, in a low voice. "She knew that your father had heart disease."

CHAPTER XL.

CONCLUSION.

At this moment Mrs. Crawford re-entered the room.

"What brings you here?" she demanded, coolly, of Carl.

"I came here because this is my father's house, madam."

"You have behaved badly to me," said Mrs. Crawford. "You have defied my authority, and brought sorrow and distress to your good father. I thought you would have the good sense to stay away."

"Do you indorse this, father?" asked Carl, turning to Dr. Crawford.

"No!" answered his father, with unwonted energy. "My house will always be your home."

"You seem to have changed your mind, Dr. Crawford," sneered his wife.

"Where did you pick up the report of Carl's being killed on the railroad?" asked the doctor, sternly.

"Peter heard it in the village," said Mrs. Crawford, carelessly.

"Did it occur to you that the sudden news might injure your husband?" asked Ashcroft.

"I spoke too impulsively. I realize too late my imprudence," said Mrs. Crawford, coolly. "Have you lost your place?" she asked, addressing Carl.

"No. I have just returned from Chicago."

His stepmother looked surprised.

"We have had a quiet time since you left us," she said. "If you value your father's health and peace of mind, you will not remain here."

"Is my presence also unwelcome?" asked Ashcroft.

"You have not treated me with respect," replied Mrs. Crawford. "If you are a gentleman, you will understand that under the circumstances it will be wise for you to take your, departure."

"Leaving my old friend to your care?"

"Yes, that will be best."

"Mr. Ashcroft, can I have a few minutes' conversation with you?" asked Carl.

"Certainly."

They left the room together, followed by an uneasy and suspicious glance from Mrs. Crawford.

Carl hurriedly communicated to his father's friend what he had learned about his stepmother.

"Mr. Cook, Peter's father, is just outside," he said. "Shall I call him in?"

"I think we had better do so, but arrange that the interview shall take place without your father's knowledge. He must not be excited. Call him in, and then summon your stepmother."

"Mrs. Crawford," said Carl, re-entering his father's room, "Mr. Ashcroft would like to have a few words with you. Can you come out?"

She followed Carl uneasily.

"What is it you want with me, sir?" she asked, frigidly.

"Let me introduce an old acquaintance of yours."

Mr. Cook, whom Mrs. Crawford had not at first observed, came forward. She drew back in dismay.

"It is some time since we met, Lucy," said Cook, quietly.

"Do you come here to make trouble?" she muttered, hoarsely.

"I come to ask for the property you took during my absence in California," he said. "I don't care to have you return to me -"

"I obtained a divorce."

"Precisely; I don't care to annul it. I am thankful that you are no longer my wife."

"I - I will see what I can do for you. Don't go near my present husband. He is in poor health, and cannot bear a shock."

"Mrs. Crawford," said Ashcroft, gravely, "if you have any idea of remaining here, in this house, give it up. I shall see that your husband's eyes are opened to your real character."

"Sir, you heard this man say that he has no claim upon me."

"That may be, but I cannot permit my friend to harbor a woman whose record is as bad as yours."

"What do you mean?" she demanded, defiantly.

"I mean that you have served a term in prison for larceny."

"It is false," she said, with trembling lips.

"It is true. I visited the prison during your term of confinement, and saw you there."

"I, too, can certify to it," said Cook. "I learned it two years after my marriage. You will understand why I am glad of the divorce."

Mrs. Crawford was silent for a moment. She realized that the battle was lost.

"Well," she said, after a pause, "I am defeated. I

thought my secret was safe, but I was mistaken. What do you propose to do with me?"

"I will tell you this evening," said Ashcroft. "One thing I can say now - you must not expect to remain in this house."

"I no longer care to do so."

A conference was held during the afternoon, Dr Crawford being told as much as was essential. It was arranged that Mrs. Crawford should have an allowance of four hundred dollars for herself and Peter if she would leave the house quietly, and never again annoy her husband. Mr. Cook offered to take Peter, but the latter preferred to remain with his mother. A private arrangement was made by which Dr. Crawford made up to Mr. Cook one-half of the sum stolen from him by his wife, and through the influence of Ashcroft, employment was found for him. He is no longer a tramp, but a man held in respect, and moderately prosperous.

Carl is still in the employ of Mr. Jennings, and his father has removed to Milford, where he and his son can live together. Next September, on his twenty-first birthday, Carl will be admitted to a junior partnership in the business, his father furnishing the necessary capital. Carl's stepmother is in Chicago, and her allowance is paid to her quarterly through a Chicago bank. She has considerable trouble with Peter, who has become less submissive as he grows older, and is unwilling to settle down to steady work. His prospects do not look very bright.

Mr. Jennings and Hannah are as much attached as ever

to Carl, and it is quite likely the manufacturer will make him his heir. Happy in the society of his son, Dr. Crawford is likely to live to a good old age, in spite of his weakness and tendency to heart disease, for happiness is a great aid to longevity.

Choose from Thousands of 1stWorldLibrary Classics By

Adolphus WilliamWard
Aesop
Agatha Christie
Alexander Aaronsohn
Alexander Kielland
Alexandre Dumas
Alfred Gatty
Alfred Ollivant
Alice Duer Miller
Alice Turner Curtis
Alice Dunbar
Ambrose Bierce
Amelia E. Barr
Andrew Lang
Andrew McFarland Davis
Anna Sewell
Annie Besant
Annie Hamilton Donnell
Annie Payson Call
Anton Chekhov
Arnold Bennett
Arthur Conan Doyle
Arthur Ransome
Atticus
B. M. Bower
Basil King
Bayard Taylor
Ben Macomber
Booth Tarkington
Bram Stoker
C. Collodi
C. E. Orr
C. M. Ingleby
Carolyn Wells
Catherine Parr Traill
Charles A. Eastman
Charles Dickens
Charles Dudley Warner
Charles Farrar Browne
Charles Ives
Charles Kingsley
Charles Lathrop Pack
Charles Whibley
Charles Willing Beale
Charlotte M. Braeme
Charlotte M.Yonge
Clair W. Hayes
Clarence Day Jr.
Clarence E. Mulford

Clemence Housman
Confucius
Cornelis DeWitt Wilcox
Cyril Burleigh
D. H. Lawrence
Daniel Defoe
David Garnett
Don Carlos Janes
Donald Keyhole
Dorothy Kilner
Dougan Clark
E. Nesbit
E.P.Roe
E. Phillips Oppenheim
Edgar Allan Poe
Edgar Rice Burroughs
Edith Wharton
Edward J. O'Biren
John Cournos
Edwin L. Arnold
Eleanor Atkins
Elizabeth Cleghorn
Gaskell
Elizabeth Von Arnim
Ellem Key
Emily Dickinson
Erasmus W. Jones
Ernie Howard Pie
Ethel Turner
Ethel Watts Mumford
Eugenie Foa
Eugene Wood
Evelyn Everett-Green
Everard Cotes
F. J. Cross
Federick Austin Ogg
Ferdinand Ossendowski
Francis Bacon
Francis Darwin
Frances Hodgson Burnett
Frank Gee Patchin
Frank Harris
Frank Jewett Mather
Frank L. Packard
Frederick Trevor Hill
Frederick Winslow Taylor
Friedrich Kerst
Friedrich Nietzsche
Fyodor Dostoyevsky

Gabrielle E. Jackson
Garrett P. Serviss
Gaston Leroux
George Ade
Geroge Bernard Shaw
George Ebers
George Eliot
George MacDonald
George Orwell
George Tucker
George W. Cable
George Wharton James
Gertrude Atherton
Grace E. King
Grant Allen
Guillermo A. Sherwell
Gulielma Zollinger
Gustav Flaubert
H. A. Cody
H. B. Irving
H. G. Wells
H. H. Munro
H. Irving Hancock
H. Rider Haggard
H. W. C. Davis
Hamilton Wright Mabie
Hans Christian Andersen
Harold Avery
Harold McGrath
Harriet Beecher Stowe
Harry Houidini
Helent Hunt Jackson
Helen Nicolay
Hendy David Thoreau
Henrik Ibsen
Henry Adams
Henry Ford
Henry Frost
Henry James
Henry Jones Ford
Henry Seton Merriman
Henry Wadsworth
Longfellow
Henry W Longfellow
Herbert A. Giles
Herbert N. Casson
Herman Hesse
Homer
Honore De Balzac

Horace Walpole
Horatio Alger, Jr.
Howard Pyle
Howard R. Garis
Hugh Lofting
Hugh Walpole
Humphry Ward
Ian Maclaren
Israel Abrahams
J.G.Austin
J. Henri Fabre
J. M. Barrie
J. Macdonald Oxley
J. S. Knowles
J. Storer Clouston
Jack London
Jacob Abbott
James Allen
James Lane Allen
James Andrews
James Baldwin
James DeMille
James Joyce
James Oliver Curwood
James Oppenheim
James Otis
Jane Austen
Jens Peter Jacobsen
Jerome K. Jerome
John Burroughs
John F. Kennedy
John Gay
John Glasworthy
John Habberton
John Joy Bell
John Milton
John Philip Sousa
Jonathan Swift
Joseph Carey
Joseph Conrad
Joseph Jacobs
Julian Hawthrone
Julies Vernes
Justin Huntly McCarthy
Kakuzo Okakura
Kenneth Grahame
Kate Langley Bosher
L. A. Abbot
L. T. Meade
L. Frank Baum
Laura Lee Hope

Laurence Housman
Leo Tolstoy
Leonid Andreyev
Lewis Carroll
Lilian Bell
Lloyd Osbourne
Louis Tracy
Louisa May Alcott
Lucy Fitch Perkins
Lucy Maud Montgomery
Lydia Miller Middleton
Lyndon Orr
M. H. Adams
Margaret E. Sangster
Margaret Vandercook
Maria Edgeworth
Maria Thompson Daviess
Mariano Azuela
Marion Polk Angellotti
Mark Overton
Mark Twain
Mary Austin
Mary Cole
Mary Rowlandson
Mary Wollstonecraft
Shelley
Max Beerbohm
Myra Kelly
Nathaniel Hawthrone
O. F. Walton
Oscar Wilde
Owen Johnson
P.G.Wodehouse
Paul and Mable Thorn
Paul G. Tomlinson
Paul Severing
Peter B. Kyne
Plato
R. Derby Holmes
R. L. Stevenson
Rabindranath Tagore
Rahul Alvares
Ralph Waldo Emmerson
Rene Descartes
Rex E. Beach
Richard Harding Davis
Richard Jefferies
Robert Barr
Robert Frost
Robert Gordon Anderson
Robert L. Drake

Robert Lansing
Robert Michael Ballantyne
Robert W. Chambers
Rosa Nouchette Carey
Ross Kay
Rudyard Kipling
Samuel B. Allison
Samuel Hopkins Adams
Sarah Bernhardt
Selma Lagerlof
Sherwood Anderson
Sigmund Freud
Standish O'Grady
Stanley Weyman
Stella Benson
Stephen Crane
Stewart Edward White
Stijn Streuvels
Swami Abhedananda
Swami Parmananda
T. S. Ackland
The Princess Der Ling
Thomas A. Janvier
Thomas A Kempis
Thomas Anderton
Thomas Bailey Aldrich
Thomas Bulfinch
Thomas De Quincey
Thomas H. Huxley
Thomas Hardy
Thomas More
Thornton W. Burgess
U. S. Grant
Valentine Williams
Victor Appleton
Virginia Woolf
Walter Scott
Washington Irving
Wilbur Lawton
Wilkie Collins
Willa Cather
Willard F. Baker
William Makepeace
Thackeray
William W. Walter
Winston Churchill
Yei Theodora Ozaki
Young E. Allison
Zane Grey

www.ingramcontent.com/pod-product-compliance
Lightning Source LLC
Chambersburg PA
CBHW020438270626
47155CB00022B/620